More Acclaim for Denis Johnson's *Jesus' Son*

"Denis Johnson's path as a writer—from poetry
to the novel to the short story—is as untypical as
his vision, but *Jesus' Son* may eventually be read
not just as a moment in his evolution but as a
distinctive turn in the history of the form. He is
doing something deeply new in these stories, and
the formal novelty brings us into a new intimacy
with the violence that is rising around us in this
country like the killing waters of a flood."

—*Atlantic Monthly*

"The narrator of these interlinked stories is a
young man, reeling from his addiction to heroin
and alcohol, his mind at once clouded and made
gorgeously lucid by these drugs. Dreams blur into
real life for this man, hallucinations mimic and
merge with reality: a state of affairs that gives Mr.
Johnson ample opportunity to display his dazzling
gift for poetic language, his natural instinct for
metaphor and wordplay."

—Michiko Kakutani,
New York Times

JESUS' SON

JESUS' SON

Stories by Denis Johnson

HARPER  PERENNIAL

NEW YORK ● LONDON ● TORONTO ● SYDNEY

First HarperPerennial edition published 1993.

Designed by Cynthia Krupat

Library of Congress Cataloging-in-Publication Data

Johnson, Denis, 1949–
    Jesus' son : stories / by Denis Johnson. —
1st HarperPerennial ed.
      p.   cm.

    Contents: Car crash while hitchhiking — Two men — Out on bail — Dundun — Work — Emergency — Dirty wedding — The other man — Happy hour — Steady hands at Seattle General — Beverly Home.
    ISBN 0-06-097577-6
    I. Title.
PS3560.03745J47   1993
813'.54 — dc20   93-8484

07 08 09 CWI 40 39 38 37

For Bob Cornfield

Stories from this collection have appeared in the
following publications: "Two Men," "Work," "Dirty
Wedding," and "Emergency" in The New Yorker; *"Car Crash*
While Hitchhiking" and "Beverly Home" in the Paris Review;
"Out on Bail" in Epoch; *"Steady Hands at Seattle General" and*
"Dundun" in Esquire; *"The Other Man" in* Big Wednesday; *"Car Crash*
While Hitchhiking" in Best American Short Stories, *1990;* "Emergency"
in Best American Short Stories, *1992.*

The author acknowledges permission to quote lyrics from
"Heroin" by Lou Reed, © *1966 Oakfield Avenue Music;*
all rights controlled and administered by Screen Gems–EMI
Music, Inc.; all rights reserved; used by permission.

CONTENTS

Car Crash While Hitchhiking / 3

Two Men / 15

Out on Bail / 35

Dundun / 45

Work / 55

Emergency / 69

Dirty Wedding / 91

The Other Man / 105

Happy Hour / 117

Steady Hands at Seattle General / 129

Beverly Home / 137

When I'm rushing on my run

And I feel just like Jesus' Son . . .

—LOU REED, *"Heroin"*

CAR CRASH
WHILE HITCHHIKING

A salesman who shared his liquor and steered while sleeping . . . A Cherokee filled with bourbon . . . A VW no more than a bubble of hashish fumes, captained by a college student . . .

And a family from Marshalltown who head-onned and killed forever a man driving west out of Bethany, Missouri . . .

. . . I rose up sopping wet from sleeping under the pouring rain, and something less than conscious, thanks to the first three of the people I've already named—the salesman and the Indian and the student—all of whom had given me drugs. At the head of the entrance ramp I waited without hope of a ride. What was the point, even, of rolling up my sleeping bag when I was too wet to be let into anybody's car? I draped it around me like a cape. The downpour raked the asphalt and gurgled in the ruts. My thoughts zoomed pitifully. The travelling salesman had fed me pills that made the linings of my veins feel scraped out. My jaw ached. I knew every raindrop by its name. I sensed everything before it happened. I knew a certain Oldsmobile would stop for me even before it slowed, and by the sweet voices of the family inside it I knew we'd have an accident in the storm.

I didn't care. They said they'd take me all the way.

The man and the wife put the little girl up front with them and left the baby in back with me and my dripping bedroll. "I'm not taking you anywhere very fast," the man said. "I've got my wife and babies here, that's why."

You are the ones, I thought. And I piled my sleeping bag against the left-hand door and slept across it, not caring whether I lived or died. The baby slept free on the seat beside me. He was about nine months old.

. . . But before any of this, that afternoon, the salesman and I had swept down into Kansas City in his luxury car. We'd developed a dangerous cynical camaraderie beginning in Texas, where he'd taken me on. We ate up his bottle of amphetamines, and every so often we pulled off the Interstate and bought another pint of Canadian

Club and a sack of ice. His car had cylindrical glass holders attached to either door and a white, leathery interior. He said he'd take me home to stay overnight with his family, but first he wanted to stop and see a woman he knew.

Under Midwestern clouds like great grey brains we left the superhighway with a drifting sensation and entered Kansas City's rush hour with a sensation of running aground. As soon as we slowed down, all the magic of travelling together burned away. He went on and on about his girlfriend. "I like this girl, I think I love this girl—but I've got two kids and a wife, and there's certain obligations there. And on top of everything else, I love my wife. I'm gifted with love. I love my kids. I love all my relatives." As he kept on, I felt jilted and sad: "I have a boat, a little sixteen-footer. I have two cars. There's room in the back yard for a swimming pool." He found his girlfriend at work. She ran a furniture store, and I lost him there.

The clouds stayed the same until night. Then, in the dark, I didn't see the storm gathering. The driver of the Volkswagen, a college man, the one who stoked my head with all the hashish, let me out beyond the city limits just as it began to rain. Never mind the speed I'd been taking, I was too overcome to stand up. I lay out in the grass off the exit ramp and woke in the middle of a puddle that had filled up around me.

And later, as I've said, I slept in the back seat while the Oldsmobile—the family from Marshalltown—splashed along through the rain. And yet I dreamed I was looking right through my eyelids, and my pulse marked off the seconds of time. The Interstate through western Missouri was, in that era, nothing more than a two-way road, most of it. When a semi truck came toward us and passed going the other way, we were lost in a blinding spray and a warfare of noises such as you get being towed through an automatic car wash. The wipers stood up and lay down across the windshield without much effect. I was exhausted, and after an hour I slept more deeply.

I'd known all along exactly what was going to happen. But the man and his wife woke me up later, denying it viciously.

"Oh—*no!*"

"NO!"

I was thrown against the back of their seat so hard that it broke. I commenced bouncing back and forth. A liquid which I knew right away was human blood flew around the car and rained down on my head. When it was over I was in the back seat again, just as I had been. I rose up and looked around. Our headlights had gone out. The radiator was hissing steadily. Beyond that, I didn't hear a thing. As far as I could tell, I was the only one conscious. As my eyes adjusted I saw that the baby was lying on its back beside me as if nothing had happened. Its eyes were open and it was feeling its cheeks with its little hands.

In a minute the driver, who'd been slumped over the wheel, sat up and peered at us. His face was smashed and dark with blood. It made my teeth hurt to look at him—but when he spoke, it didn't sound as if any of his teeth were broken.

"What happened?"

"We had a wreck," he said.

"The baby's okay," I said, although I had no idea how the baby was.

He turned to his wife.

"Janice," he said. "Janice, Janice!"

"Is she okay?"

"She's dead!" he said, shaking her angrily.

"No, she's not." I was ready to deny everything myself now.

Their little girl was alive, but knocked out. She whimpered in her sleep. But the man went on shaking his wife.

"Janice!" he hollered.

His wife moaned.

"She's not dead," I said, clambering from the car and running away.

"She won't wake up," I heard him say.

I was standing out here in the night, with the baby, for some reason, in my arms. It must have still been raining, but I remember nothing about the weather. We'd collided with another car on what I now perceived was a two-lane bridge. The water beneath us was invisible in the dark.

Moving toward the other car I began to hear rasping, metallic snores. Somebody was flung halfway out the passenger door, which was open, in the posture of one hanging from a trapeze by his ankles. The car had been broadsided, smashed so flat that no room was left inside it even for this person's legs, to say nothing of a driver or any other passengers. I just walked right on past.

Headlights were coming from far off. I made for the head of the bridge, waving them to a stop with one arm and clutching the baby to my shoulder with the other.

It was a big semi, grinding its gears as it decelerated. The driver rolled down his window and I shouted up at him, "There's a wreck. Go for help."

"I can't turn around here," he said.

He let me and the baby up on the passenger side, and we just sat there in the cab, looking at the wreckage in his headlights.

"Is everybody dead?" he asked.

"I can't tell who is and who isn't," I admitted.

He poured himself a cup of coffee from a thermos and switched off all but his parking lights.

"What time is it?"

"Oh, it's around quarter after three," he said.

By his manner he seemed to endorse the idea of not doing anything about this. I was relieved and tearful. I'd thought something was required of me, but I hadn't wanted to find out what it was.

When another car showed coming in the opposite direction, I thought I should talk to them. "Can you keep the baby?" I asked the truck driver.

"You'd better hang on to him," the driver said. "It's a boy, isn't it?"

"Well, I think so," I said.

The man hanging out of the wrecked car was still alive as I passed, and I stopped, grown a little more used to the idea now of how really badly broken he was, and made sure there was nothing I could do. He was snoring loudly and rudely. His blood bubbled out of his mouth with every breath. He wouldn't be taking many more. I knew that, but he didn't, and therefore I looked down into the great pity of a person's life on this earth. I don't mean that we all end up dead, that's not the great pity. I mean that he couldn't tell me what he was dreaming, and I couldn't tell him what was real.

Before too long there were cars backed up for a ways at either end of the bridge, and headlights giving a night-game atmosphere to the steaming rubble, and ambulances and cop cars nudging through so that the air pulsed with color. I didn't talk to anyone. My secret was that in this short while I had gone from being the president of this tragedy to being a faceless onlooker at a gory wreck. At some point an officer learned that I was one of the passengers, and took my statement. I don't remember any of this, except that he told me, "Put out your cigarette." We paused in our conversation to watch the dying man being loaded into the ambulance. He was still alive, still dreaming obscenely. The blood ran off him in strings. His knees jerked and his head rattled.

There was nothing wrong with me, and I hadn't seen anything, but the policeman had to question me and take me to the hospital anyway. The word came over his car radio that the man was now dead, just as we came under the awning of the emergency-room entrance.

I stood in a tiled corridor with my wet sleeping bag bunched against the wall beside me, talking to a man from the local funeral home.

The doctor stopped to tell me I'd better have an X-ray.

"No."

"Now would be the time. If something turns up later . . ."

"There's nothing wrong with me."

Down the hall came the wife. She was glorious, burning. She didn't know yet that her husband was dead. We knew. That's what gave her such power over us. The doctor took her into a room with a desk at the end of the hall, and from under the closed door a slab of brilliance radiated as if, by some stupendous process, diamonds were being incinerated in there. What a pair of lungs! She shrieked as I imagined an eagle would shriek. It felt wonderful to be alive to hear it! I've gone looking for that feeling everywhere.

"There's nothing wrong with me"—I'm surprised I let those words out. But it's always been my tendency to lie to doctors, as if good health consisted only of the ability to fool them.

Some years later, one time when I was admitted to the Detox at Seattle General Hospital, I took the same tack.

"Are you hearing unusual sounds or voices?" the doctor asked.

"Help us, oh God, it hurts," the boxes of cotton screamed.

"Not exactly," I said.

"Not exactly," he said. "Now, what does that mean."

"I'm not ready to go into all that," I said. A yellow bird fluttered close to my face, and my muscles grabbed. Now I was flopping like a fish. When I squeezed shut my eyes, hot tears exploded from the sockets. When I opened them, I was on my stomach.

"How did the room get so white?" I asked.

A beautiful nurse was touching my skin. "These are vitamins," she said, and drove the needle in.

It was raining. Gigantic ferns leaned over us. The forest drifted down a hill. I could hear a creek rushing down among rocks. And you, you ridiculous people, you expect me to help you.

TWO MEN

I met the first man as I was going home from a dance at the Veterans of Foreign Wars Hall. I was being taken out of the dance by my two good friends. I had forgotten my friends had come with me, but there they were. Once again I hated the two of them. The three of us had formed a group based on something erroneous, some basic misunderstanding that hadn't yet come to light, and so we kept on in one another's company, going to bars and having conversations. Generally one of these false coalitions died after a day or a day and a half, but this one had lasted more than a year. Later on one of them got hurt when we were burglarizing a pharmacy, and the other two of us dropped him bleeding at the back entrance of the hospital and he was arrested and all the bonds were dissolved. We bailed him out later, and still later all the charges against him were dropped,

but we'd torn open our chests and shown our
cowardly hearts, and you can never stay friends
after something like that.

This evening at the Veterans of Foreign Wars
Hall I'd backed a woman up behind the huge air-
conditioning unit while we were dancing, and
kissed her and unbuttoned her pants and put my
hand down the front of them. She'd been married
to a friend of mine until about a year before, and
I'd always thought we'd probably get mixed up
together, but her boyfriend, a mean, skinny, in-
telligent man who I happened to feel inferior to,
came around the corner of the machine and glow-
ered at us and told her to go out and get in the
car. I was afraid he'd take some kind of action,
but he disappeared just as quickly as she did.
The rest of the evening I wondered, every second,
if he would come back with some friends and
make something painful and degrading happen.
I was carrying a gun, but it wasn't as if I would
actually have used it. It was so cheap, I was sure
it would explode in my hands if I ever pulled the
trigger. So it could only add to my humiliation
—afterwards people, usually men talking to
women in my imagination, would say, "He had
a gun, but he never even took it out of his pants."
I drank as much as I could until the western

combo stopped singing and playing and the lights came up.

My two friends and I went to get into my little green Volkswagen, and we discovered the man I started to tell you about, the first man, sleeping deeply in the back seat.

"Who's this?" I asked my two friends. But they'd never seen him before either.

We got him awake, and he sat up. He was something of a hulk, not so tall that his head hit the roof, but really broad, with a thick face and close-cropped hair. He wouldn't get out of the car.

This man pointed to his own ears and to his mouth, signalling that he couldn't hear or talk.

"What do you do in a situation like this?" I said.

"Well, I'm getting in. Move over," Tom said to the man, and got in the back seat with him.

Richard and I got in the front. We all three turned to the new companion.

He pointed straight ahead and then laid his cheek on his hands, indicating beddy-bye. "He just wants a ride home," I guessed.

"So?" Tom said. "Give him a ride home." Tom had such sharp features that his moods looked even worse than they were.

Using sign language, the passenger showed us where to take him. Tom relayed the directions, because I couldn't see the man while I was driving. "Take a right—a left here—he wants you to slow down—he's looking for the place—" and like that.

We drove with the windows down. The mild spring evening, after several frozen winter months, was like a foreigner breathing in our faces. We took our passenger to a residential street where the buds were forcing themselves out of the tips of branches and the seeds were moaning in the gardens.

He was as bulky as an ape, we saw when he was out of the car, and dangled his hands as if he might suddenly go down and start walking on his knuckles. He glided up the walk of one particular home and banged on the door. A light went on in the second story, the curtain moved, and the light went out. He was back at the car, thumping on the roof with his hand, before I got the thing in gear to pull away and leave him.

He draped himself over the front of my VW and seemed to pass out.

"Wrong house, maybe," Richard suggested.

"I can't navigate with him like that," I said.

"Take off," Richard said, "and slam on the brakes."

"The brakes aren't working," Tom told Richard.

"The emergency brake works," I assured everybody.

Tom had no patience. "All you have to do is move this car, and he'll fall off."

"I don't want to hurt him."

We ended it by hefting him into the back seat, where he slumped against the window.

Now we were stuck with him again. Tom laughed sarcastically. We all three lit cigarettes.

"Here comes Caplan to shoot off my legs," I said, looking in terror at a car as it came around the corner and then passed by. "I was sure it was him," I said as its taillights disappeared down the block.

"Are you still all worried about Alsatia?"

"I was kissing her."

"There's no law against that," Richard said.

"It's not her lawyer I'm worried about."

"I don't think Caplan's that serious about her. Not enough to kill you, or anything like that."

"What do you think about all this?" I asked our drunken buddy.

He started snoring ostentatiously.

"This guy isn't really deaf—are you, hey," Tom said.

"What do we do with him?"

"Take him home with us."

"Not me," I said.

"One of us should, anyway."

"He lives right there," I insisted. "You could tell by the way he knocked."

I got out of the car.

I went to the house and rang the doorbell and stepped back off the porch, looking up at the overhead window in the dark. The white curtain moved again, and a woman said something.

All of her was invisible except the shadow of her hand on the curtain's border. "If you don't take him off our street I'm calling the police." I was so flooded with yearning I thought it would drown me. Her voice broke off and floated down.

"I've got the phone now. Now I'm dialling," she called down softly.

I thought I heard a car's engine somewhere not too far away. I ran back to the street.

"What is it?" Richard said as I got in.

Headlights came around the corner. A spasm ran through me so hard it shook the car. "Jesus," I said. The interior filled up with light so that for two seconds you could have read a book. The shadows of dust streaks on the windshield striped Tom's face. "It's nobody," Richard said, and the dark closed up again as whoever it was went past.

"Caplan doesn't know where you are, anyway."

The jolt of fear had burned all the red out of my blood. I was like rubber. "I'll go after him, then. Let's just have it out."

"Maybe he doesn't care or—I don't know. What do I know?" Tom said. "Why are we even talking about him?"

"Maybe he forgives you," Richard said.

"Oh God, if he does, then we're comrades and so on, forever," I said. "All I'm asking is just punish me and get it over with."

The passenger wasn't defeated. He gestured all over the place, touching his forehead and his armpits and gyrating somewhat in place, like a baseball coach signalling his players. "Look," I said. "I know you can talk. Don't act like we're stupid."

He directed us through this part of town and then over near the train tracks where hardly anybody lived. Here and there were shacks with dim lights inside them, sunk to the bottom of all this darkness. But the house he had me stop in front of got no light except from the streetlamp. Nothing happened when I honked the horn. The man we were helping just sat there. All this time he'd voiced plenty of desires but hadn't said a word. More and more he began to seem like somebody's dog.

"I'll take a look," I told him, making my voice cruel.

It was a small wooden house with two posts for a clothesline out front. The grass had grown up and been crushed by the snows and then uncovered by the thaw. Without bothering to knock I went around to the window and looked in. There was one chair all by itself at an oval table. The house looked abandoned, no curtains, no rugs. All over the floor there were shiny things I thought might be spent flashbulbs or empty bullet casings. But it was dark and nothing was clear. I peered around until my eyes were tired and I thought I could make out designs all over the floor like the chalk outlines of victims or markings for strange rituals.

"Why don't you go in there?" I asked the guy when I got back to the car. "Just go look. You faker, you loser."

He held up one finger. *One.*

"What."

One. One.

"He wants to go one more place," Richard said.

"We already went one more place. This place right here. And it was just bogus."

"What do you want to do?" Tom said.

"Oh, let's just take him wherever he wants to

go." I didn't want to go home. My wife was different than she used to be, and we had a six-month-old baby I was afraid of, a little son.

The next place we took him to stood all by itself out on the Old Highway. I'd been out this road more than once, a little farther every time, and I'd never found anything that made me happy. Some of my friends had had a farm out here, but the police had raided the place and put them all in jail.

This house didn't seem to be part of a farm. It was about two-tenths of a mile off the Old Highway, its front porch edged right up against the road. When we stopped in front of it and turned off the engine, we heard music coming from inside—jazz. It sounded sophisticated and lonely.

We all went up to the porch with the silent man. He knocked on the door. Tom, Richard, and I flanked him at a slight, a very subtle distance.

As soon as the door opened, he pushed his way inside. We followed him in and stopped, but he headed right into the next room.

We didn't get any farther inside than the kitchen. The next room past that was dim and blue-lit, and inside it, through the doorway, we saw a loft, almost a gigantic bunk bed, in which several ghost-complected women were lying around. One just like those came through the door from that room and stood looking at the three of us with her mascara blurred and her lipstick kissed away. She wore a skirt but not a blouse, just a white bra like someone in an undies ad in a teenage magazine. But she was older than that. Looking at her I thought of going out in the fields with my wife back when we were so in love we didn't know what it was.

She wiped her nose, a sleepy gesture. Inside of two seconds she was closely attended by a black man slapping the palm of his hand with a pair of gloves, a very large man looking blindly down at me with the invulnerable smile of someone on dope.

The young woman said, "If you'd called ahead, we would've encouraged you not to bring him."

Her companion was delighted. "That's a beautiful way of saying it."

In the room behind her the man we'd brought stood like a bad sculpture, posing unnaturally with his shoulders wilting, as if he couldn't lug his gigantic hands any farther.

"What the hell is his problem?" Richard asked.

"It doesn't matter what his problem is, until he's fully understood it himself," the man said.

Tom laughed, in a way.

"What does he do?" Richard asked the girl.

"He's a real good football player. Or anyhow he was." Her face was tired. She couldn't have cared less.

"He's still good. He's still on the team," the black man said.

"He's not even in school."

"But he could get back on the team if he was."

"But he'll never be in school because he's fucked, man. And so are you."

He flicked one of his gloves back and forth. "I know that now, thank you, baby."

"You dropped your other glove," she said.

"Thank you, babe, I know that, too," he said.

A big muscular boy with fresh cheeks and a blond flattop came over and joined us. I felt he was the host, because he gripped the handle of a green beer mug almost the size of a wastepaper basket with a swastika and a dollar sign painted on it. This personalized touch made him seem right at home, like Hugh Hefner circulating around the *Playboy* cocktail parties in his pajamas.

He smiled at me and shook his head. "He can't stay. Tammy doesn't want him here."

"Okay, whoever Tammy is," I said. Around these strange people I felt hungry. I smelled some kind of debauchery, the whiff of a potion that would banish everything plaguing me.

"Now would be a good time to take him out of here," the big host said.

"What's his name, anyway?"

"Stan."

"Stan. Is he really deaf?"

The girl snorted.

The boy laughed and said, "That's a good one."

Richard punched my arm and glanced at the door, indicating we should go. I realized that he and Tom were afraid of these people; and then I was, too. Not that they'd do anything to us; but around them we felt almost like stupid failures.

The woman hurt me. She looked so soft and perfect, like a mannequin made of flesh, flesh all the way through.

"Let's ditch him—right now," I cried, hurrying out the door.

I was already in the driver's seat, and Tom and Richard were halfway down the walk, before Stan came out of the house. "Lose him! Lose him!" Tom yelled, getting in after Richard, but the man already had a grip on the door handle by the time I'd started pulling away.

I goosed it, but he wouldn't give up. He even managed to keep a slight lead and look around

right at me through the front window, keeping
up a psychotic eye contact and wearing a sar-
castic smile, as if to say he'd be with us forever,
running faster and faster, puffing out clouds of
breath. After fifty yards, as we neared the stop
sign at the main road, I really gunned it, hoping
to wrench free, but all I did was yank him right
into the stop sign. His head hit it first, and the
post broke off like a green stalk and he fell,
sprawling all over it. The wood must have been
rotten. Lucky for him.

We left him behind, a man staggering around
a crossroads where a stop sign used to stand. "I
thought I knew everyone in town," Tom said,
"but those people are completely new to me."

"They used to be jocks, but now they're
heads," Richard said.

"Football people. I didn't know they ever got
like that." Tom was looking backward, down the
road.

I stopped the car, and we all looked back. A
quarter mile behind us, Stan paused among the
fields in the starlight, in the posture of somebody
who had a pounding hangover or was trying to
fit his head back onto his neck. But it wasn't just
his head, it was all of him that had been cut off
and thrown away. No wonder he didn't hear or
speak, no wonder he didn't have anything to do

with words. Everything along those lines was used up.

We stared at him and felt like old maids. He, on the other hand, was the bride of Death.

We took off. "Never got him to say a word."

All the way back to town, Tom and I criticized him.

"You just don't realize. Being a cheerleader, being on the team, it doesn't guarantee anything. Anybody can take a turn for the worse," said Richard, who'd been a high school quarterback or something himself.

As soon as we hit the city limits, where the chain of streetlamps began, I was back to wondering about and fearing Caplan.

"I'd better just go after him, instead of waiting," I suggested to Tom.

"Who?"

"Who do you think?"

"Will you forget it? It's over. Seriously."

"Yeah. Okay, okay."

We drove up Burlington Street. We passed the all-night gas station at the corner of Clinton. A man was handing money to the attendant, both of them standing by his car in an eerie sulfur light—those sodium-arc lamps were new in our town then—and the pavement around them was spangled with oil stains that looked green, while his old Ford was no color at all. "You know who that was?" I told Tom and Richard. "That was Thatcher."

I made a U-turn as quickly as I could.

"So what?" Tom said.

"So this," I said, producing the .32 I'd never fired.

Richard laughed, I don't know why. Tom laid his hands on his knees and sighed.

Thatcher was back in his car by this time. I pulled up to the pumps going the other direction, and rolled down my window. "I bought one of those phony kilos you were selling for two-ten right around last New Year's. You don't know me, because what's-his-name was selling them for you." I doubt he heard me. I showed him the pistol.

Thatcher's tires gave a yip as he took off in his corroded Falcon. I didn't think I'd catch him in the VW, but I spun it around after him. "The stuff he sold me was a burn," I said.

"Didn't you try it first?" Richard said.

"It was weird stuff."

"Well, if you tried it," he said.

"It seemed all right, and then it wasn't. It wasn't just me. Everybody else said so, too."

"He's losing you." Thatcher had hooked very suddenly between two buildings.

I couldn't find him as we exited the alley onto another street. But up ahead I saw a patch of old snow go pink in somebody's brake lights.

"He's turned that corner," I said.

When we rounded the building we found his car parked, empty, in back of an apartment house. A light went on in one of the apartments, and then went off.

"I'm two seconds behind him." The feeling that he was afraid of me was invigorating. I left the VW in the middle of the parking lot with the door open and the engine on and the headlights burning.

Tom and Richard were behind me as I ran up the first flight of stairs and banged on the door with the gun. I knew I was in the right place. I banged again. A woman in a white nightgown opened it, backing away and saying, "Don't. All right. All right. All right."

"Thatcher must have told you to answer, or you never would've opened the door," I said.

"Jim? He's out of town." She had long black hair in a ponytail. Her eyeballs were positively shaking in her head.

"Get him," I said.

"He's in California."

"He's in the bedroom." I backed her up, moving toward her behind the mouth of the gun.

"I've got two kids here," she begged.

"I don't care! Get on the floor!"

She got down, and I pushed the side of her face into the rug and laid the gun against her temple.

Thatcher was going to come out or I didn't know what. "I've got her on the floor in here!" I called back toward the bedroom.

"My kids are sleeping," she said. The tears ran out of her eyes and over the bridge of her nose.

Suddenly and stupidly, Richard walked right down the hall and into the bedroom. Flagrant, self-destructive gestures—he was known for them.

"There's nobody back here but two little kids."

Tom joined him. "He climbed out the window," he called back to me.

I took two steps over to the living-room window and looked down onto the parking lot. I couldn't tell for certain, but it looked like Thatcher's car was gone.

The woman hadn't moved. She just lay there on the rug.

"He's really not here," she said.

I knew he wasn't. "I don't care. You're going to be sorry," I said.

OUT ON BAIL

I saw Jack Hotel in an olive-green three-piece suit, with his blond hair combed back and his face shining and suffering. People who knew him were buying him drinks as quickly as he could drink them down at the Vine, people who were briefly acquainted, people who couldn't even remember if they knew him or not. It was a sad, exhilarating occasion. He was being tried for armed robbery. He'd come from the courthouse during the lunch recess. He'd looked in his lawyer's eyes and fathomed that it would be a short trial. According to a legal math that only the mind of the accused has strength to pursue, he guessed the minimum in this case would have to be twenty-five years.

It was so horrible it could only have been a joke. I myself couldn't remember ever having met anybody who'd actually lived that long on the earth. As for Hotel, he was eighteen or nineteen.

This situation had been a secret until now, like a terminal disease. I was envious that he could keep such a secret, and frightened that somebody as weak as Hotel should be gifted with something so grand that he couldn't even bring himself to brag about it. Hotel had taken me for a hundred dollars once and I always talked maliciously about him behind his back, but I'd known him ever since he'd appeared, when he was fifteen or sixteen. I was surprised and hurt, even miserable, that he hadn't seen fit to let me in on his trouble. It seemed to foretell that these people would never be my friends.

Right now his hair was so clean and blond for once that it seemed the sun was shining on him even in this subterranean region.

I looked down the length of the Vine. It was a long, narrow place, like a train car that wasn't going anywhere. The people all seemed to have escaped from someplace—I saw plastic hospital name bracelets on several wrists. They were trying to pay for their drinks with counterfeit money they'd made themselves, in Xerox machines.

"It happened a long time ago," he said.

"What did you do? Who did you rip off?"

"It was last year. It was last year." He laughed

at himself for calling down a brand of justice that would hound him for that long.

"Who did you rip off, Hotel?"

"Aah, don't ask me. Shit. Fuck. God." He turned and started talking to somebody else.

The Vine was different every day. Some of the most terrible things that had happened to me in my life had happened in here. But like the others I kept coming back.

And with each step my heart broke for the person I would never find, the person who'd love me. And then I would remember I had a wife at home who loved me, or later that my wife had left me and I was terrified, or again later that I had a beautiful alcoholic girlfriend who would make me happy forever. But every time I entered the place there were veiled faces promising everything and then clarifying quickly into the dull, the usual, looking up at me and making the same mistake.

That night I sat in a booth across from Kid Williams, a former boxer. His black hands were lumpy and mutilated. I always had the feeling he might suddenly reach out his hands and strangle me to death. He spoke in two voices. He was in his fifties. He'd wasted his entire life. Such people were very dear to those of us who'd wasted only a few years. With Kid Williams sitting across from you it was nothing to contemplate going on like this for another month or two.

I wasn't exaggerating about those hospital name bands. Kid Williams was wearing one on his wrist. He'd just come over the wall from Detox. "Buy me a drink, buy me a drink," he said in his high voice. Then he frowned and said in his low voice, "I come down here for just a short time," and brightening, in his high voice: "I wanted to see you-all! Buy me one now, because I don't have my purse, my wallet, they took all my money. They thiefs." He grabbed at the barmaid like a child after a toy. All he was wearing was a nightshirt tucked into his pants and hospital slippers made of green paper.

Suddenly I remembered that Hotel himself, or somebody connected with him, had told me weeks ago that Hotel was in trouble for armed robbery. He'd stolen drugs and money at gunpoint from some college students who'd been selling a lot of cocaine, and they'd decided to turn him in. I'd forgotten I'd ever heard about it.

And then, as if to twist my life even further, I realized that all the celebrating that afternoon hadn't been Hotel's farewell party after all, but his welcome home. He'd been acquitted. His lawyer had managed to clear him on the curious grounds that he'd been trying to defend the com-

munity against the influence of these drug deal-
ers. Completely confused as to who the real
criminals were in this case, the jury had voted
to wash their hands of everybody and they let
him off. That had been the meaning of the conversation I'd had with him that afternoon, but I
hadn't understood what was happening at all.

There were many moments in the Vine like that
one—where you might think today was yesterday, and yesterday was tomorrow, and so on.
Because we all believed we were tragic, and we
drank. We had that helpless, destined feeling.
We would die with handcuffs on. We would be
put a stop to, and it wouldn't be our fault. So
we imagined. And yet we were always being found
innocent for ridiculous reasons.

Hotel was given back the rest of his life, the
twenty-five years and more. The police promised
him, because they were so bitter about his good
luck, that if he didn't leave town they would make
him sorry he'd stayed. He stuck it out a while,
but fought with his girlfriend and left—he held
jobs in Denver, Reno, points west—and then
within a year turned up again because he couldn't
keep away from her.

Now he was twenty, twenty-one years old.

The Vine had been torn down. Urban renewal
had changed all the streets. As for me, my girl-

friend and I had split up, but we couldn't keep away from each other.

One night she and I fought, and I walked the streets till the bars opened in the morning. I just went into any old place.

Jack Hotel was beside me in the mirror, drinking. There were some others there exactly like the two of us, and we were comforted.

Sometimes what I wouldn't give to have us sitting in a bar again at 9:00 a.m. telling lies to one another, far from God.

Hotel had fought with his girlfriend, too. He'd walked the streets as I had. Now we matched each other drink for drink until we both ran out of money.

I knew of an apartment building where a dead tenant's Social Security checks were still being delivered. I'd been stealing them every month for half a year, always with trepidation, always delaying a couple of days after their arrival, always thinking I'd find an honest way to make a few dollars, always believing I was an honest person who shouldn't be doing things like that, always delaying because I was afraid this time I'd be caught.

Hotel went along with me while I stole the check. I forged the signature and signed it over to him, under his true name, so that he could cash it at a supermarket. I believe his true name was George Hoddel. It's German. We bought heroin with the money and split the heroin down the middle.

Then he went looking for his girlfriend, and I went looking for mine, knowing that when there were drugs around, she surrendered.

But I was in a bad condition—drunk, and having missed a night's sleep. As soon as the stuff entered my system, I passed out. Two hours went by without my noticing.

I felt I'd only blinked my eyes, but when I opened them my girlfriend and a Mexican neighbor were working on me, doing everything they could to bring me back. The Mexican was saying, "There, he's coming around now."

We lived in a tiny, dirty apartment. When I realized how long I'd been out and how close I'd come to leaving it forever, our little home seemed to glitter like cheap jewelry. I was overjoyed not to be dead. Generally the closest I ever came to wondering about the meaning of it all was to consider that I must be the victim of a joke. There was no touching the hem of mystery, no little occasion when any of us thought—well, speaking for myself only, I suppose—that our lungs were filled with light, or anything like that. I had a moment's glory that night, though. I was certain

I was here in this world because I couldn't tolerate any other place.

As for Hotel, who was in exactly the same shape I was and carrying just as much heroin, but who didn't have to share it with his girlfriend, because he couldn't find her that day: he took himself to a rooming house down at the end of Iowa Avenue, and he overdosed, too. He went into a deep sleep, and to the others there he looked quite dead.

The people with him, all friends of ours, monitored his breathing by holding a pocket mirror under his nostrils from time to time, making sure that points of mist appeared on the glass. But after a while they forgot about him, and his breath failed without anybody's noticing. He simply went under. He died.

I am still alive.

DUNDUN

I went out to the farmhouse where Dundun lived to get some pharmaceutical opium from him, but I was out of luck.

He greeted me as he was coming out into the front yard to go to the pump, wearing new cowboy boots and a leather vest, with his flannel shirt hanging out over his jeans. He was chewing on a piece of gum.

"McInnes isn't feeling too good today. I just shot him."

"You mean killed him?"

"I didn't mean to."

"Is he really dead?"

"No. He's sitting down."

"But he's alive."

"Oh, sure, he's alive. He's sitting down now in the back room."

Dundun went on over to the pump and started working the handle.

I went around the house and in through the back. The room just through the back door smelled of dogs and babies. Beatle stood in the opposite doorway. She watched me come in. Leaning against the wall was Blue, smoking a cigarette and scratching her chin thoughtfully. Jack Hotel was over at an old desk, setting fire to a pipe the bowl of which was wrapped in tinfoil.

When they saw it was only me, the three of them resumed looking at McInnes, who sat on the couch all alone, with his left hand resting gently on his belly.

"Dundun shot him?" I asked.

"Somebody shot somebody," Hotel said.

Dundun came in behind me carrying some water in a china cup and a bottle of beer and said to McInnes: "Here."

"*I* don't want that," McInnes said.

"Okay. Well, here, then." Dundun offered him the rest of his beer.

"No thanks."

I was worried. "Aren't you taking him to the hospital or anything?"

"Good idea," Beatle said sarcastically.

"We started to," Hotel explained, "but we ran into the corner of the shed out there."

I looked out the side window. This was Tim Bishop's farm. Tim Bishop's Plymouth, I saw, which was a very nice old grey-and-red sedan, had sideswiped the shed and replaced one of the corner posts, so that the post lay on the ground and the car now held up the shed's roof.

"The front windshield is in millions of bits," Hotel said.

"How'd you end up way over there?"

"Everything was completely out of hand," Hotel said.

"Where's Tim, anyway?"

"He's not here," Beatle said.

Hotel passed me the pipe. It was hashish, but it was pretty well burned up already.

"How you doing?" Dundun asked McInnes.

"I can feel it right here. It's just stuck in the muscle."

Dundun said, "It's not bad. The cap didn't explode right, I think."

"It misfired."

"It misfired a little bit, yeah."

Hotel asked me, "Would you take him to the hospital in your car?"

"Okay," I said.

"I'm coming, too," Dundun said.

"Have you got any of the opium left?" I asked him.

"No," he said. "That was a birthday present. I used it all up."

"When's your birthday?" I asked him.

"Today."

"You shouldn't have used it all up before your birthday, then," I told him angrily.

But I was happy about this chance to be of use. I wanted to be the one who saw it through and got McInnes to the doctor without a wreck. People would talk about it, and I hoped I would be liked.

In the car were Dundun, McInnes, and myself.

This was Dundun's twenty-first birthday. I'd met him in the Johnson County facility during the only few days I'd ever spent in jail, around the time of my eighteenth Thanksgiving. I was the older of us by a month or two. As for McInnes, he'd been around forever, and in fact, I, myself, was married to one of his old girlfriends.

We took off as fast as I could go without bouncing the shooting victim around too heavily.

Dundun said, "What about the brakes? You get them working?"

"The emergency brake does. That's enough."

"What about the radio?" Dundun punched the button, and the radio came on making an emission like a meat grinder.

He turned it off and then on, and now it burbled like a machine that polishes stones all night.

"How about you?" I asked McInnes. "Are you comfortable?"

"What do you think?" McInnes said.

It was a long straight road through dry fields as far as a person could see. You'd think the sky didn't have any air in it, and the earth was made of paper. Rather than moving, we were just getting smaller and smaller.

What can be said about those fields? There were blackbirds circling above their own shadows, and beneath them the cows stood around smelling one another's butts. Dundun spat his gum out the window while digging in his shirt pocket for his Winstons. He lit a Winston with a match. That was all there was to say.

"We'll never get off this road," I said.

"What a lousy birthday," Dundun said.

McInnes was white and sick, holding himself tenderly. I'd seen him like that once or twice even when he hadn't been shot. He had a bad case of hepatitis that often gave him a lot of pain.

"Do you promise not to tell them anything?" Dundun was talking to McInnes.

"I don't think he hears you," I said.

"Tell them it was an accident, okay?"

McInnes said nothing for a long moment. Finally he said, "Okay."

"Promise?" Dundun said.

But McInnes said nothing. Because he was dead.

Dundun looked at me with tears in his eyes. "What do you say?"

"What do you mean, what do I say? Do you think I'm here because I know all about this stuff?"

"He's dead."

"All *right*. I *know* he's dead."

"Throw him out of the car."

"Damn right throw him out of the car," I said. "I'm not taking him anywhere now."

For a moment I fell asleep, right while I was driving. I had a dream in which I was trying to tell someone something and they kept interrupting, a dream about frustration.

"I'm glad he's dead," I told Dundun. "He's the one who started everybody calling me Fuckhead."

Dundun said, "Don't let it get you down."

We whizzed along down through the skeleton remnants of Iowa.

"I wouldn't mind working as a hit man," Dundun said.

Glaciers had crushed this region in the time before history. There'd been a drought for years, and a bronze fog of dust stood over the plains.

The soybean crop was dead again, and the failed, wilted cornstalks were laid out on the ground like rows of underthings. Most of the farmers didn't even plant anymore. All the false visions had been erased. It felt like the moment before the Savior comes. And the Savior did come, but we had to wait a long time.

Dundun tortured Jack Hotel at the lake outside of Denver. He did this to get information about a stolen item, a stereo belonging to Dundun's girlfriend, or perhaps to his sister. Later, Dundun beat a man almost to death with a tire iron right on the street in Austin, Texas, for which he'll also someday have to answer, but now he is, I think, in the state prison in Colorado.

Will you believe me when I tell you there was kindness in his heart? His left hand didn't know what his right hand was doing. It was only that certain important connections had been burned through. If I opened up your head and ran a hot soldering iron around in your brain, I might turn you into someone like that.

WORK

I'd been staying at the Holiday Inn with my girlfriend, honestly the most beautiful woman I'd ever known, for three days under a phony name, shooting heroin. We made love in the bed, ate steaks at the restaurant, shot up in the john, puked, cried, accused one another, begged of one another, forgave, promised, and carried one another to heaven.

But there was a fight. I stood outside the motel hitchhiking, dressed up in a hurry, shirtless under my jacket, with the wind crying through my earring. A bus came. I climbed aboard and sat on the plastic seat while the things of our city turned in the windows like the images in a slot machine.

Once, as we stood arguing at a streetcorner, I punched her in the stomach. She doubled over and broke down crying. A car full of young college men stopped beside us.

"She's feeling sick," I told them.

"Bullshit," one of them said. "You elbowed her right in the *gut*."

"He did, he did, he did," she said, weeping.

I don't remember what I said to them. I remember loneliness crushing first my lungs, then my heart, then my balls. They put her in the car with them and drove away.

But she came back.

This morning, after the fight, after sitting on the bus for several blocks with a thoughtless, red mind, I jumped down and walked into the Vine.

The Vine was still and cold. Wayne was the only customer. His hands were shaking. He couldn't lift his glass.

I put my left hand on Wayne's shoulder, and with my right, opiated and steady, I brought his shot of bourbon to his lips.

"How would you feel about making some money?" he asked me.

"I was just going to go over here in the corner and nod out," I informed him.

"I decided," he said, "in my mind, to make some money."

"So what?" I said.

"Come with me," he begged.

"You mean you need a ride."

"I have the tools," he said. "All we need is that sorry-ass car of yours to get around in."

We found my sixty-dollar Chevrolet, the finest and best thing I ever bought, considering the price, in the streets near my apartment. I liked that car. It was the kind of thing you could bang into a phone pole with and nothing would happen at all.

Wayne cradled his burlap sack of tools in his lap as we drove out of town to where the fields bunched up into hills and then dipped down toward a cool river mothered by benevolent clouds.

All the houses on the riverbank—a dozen or so—were abandoned. The same company, you could tell, had built them all, and then painted them four different colors. The windows in the lower stories were empty of glass. We passed alongside them and I saw that the ground floors of these buildings were covered with silt. Sometime back a flood had run over the banks, cancelling everything. But now the river was flat and slow. Willows stroked the waters with their hair.

"Are we doing a burglary?" I asked Wayne.

"You can't burgulate a forgotten, empty house," he said, horrified at my stupidity.

I didn't say anything.

"This is a salvage job," he said. "Pull up to that one, right about there."

The house we parked in front of just had a terrible feeling about it. I knocked.

"Don't do that," Wayne said. "It's stupid."

Inside, our feet kicked up the silt the river had left here. The watermark wandered the walls of the downstairs about three feet above the floor. Straight, stiff grass lay all over the place in bunches, as if someone had stretched them there to dry.

Wayne used a pry bar, and I had a shiny hammer with a blue rubber grip. We put the pry points in the seams of the wall and started tearing away the Sheetrock. It came loose with a noise like old men coughing. Whenever we exposed some of the wiring in its white plastic jacket, we ripped it free of its connections, pulled it out, and bunched it up. That's what we were after. We intended to sell the copper wire for scrap.

By the time we were on the second floor, I could see we were going to make some money. But I was getting tired. I dropped the hammer, went to the bathroom. I was sweaty and thirsty. But of course the water didn't work.

I went back to Wayne, standing in one of two small empty bedrooms, and started dancing

around and pounding the walls, breaking
through the Sheetrock and making a giant racket,
until the hammer got stuck. Wayne ignored this
misbehavior.

I was catching my breath.

I asked him, "Who owned these houses, do you
think?"

He stopped doing anything. "This is my
house."

"It is?"

"It was."

He gave the wire a long, smooth yank, a gesture
full of the serenity of hatred, popping its staples
and freeing it into the room.

We balled up big gobs of wire in the center of
each room, working for over an hour. I boosted
Wayne through the trapdoor into the attic, and
he pulled me up after him, both of us sweating
and our pores leaking the poisons of drink, which
smelled like old citrus peelings, and we made a
mound of white-jacketed wire in the top of his
former home, pulling it up out of the floor.

I felt weak. I had to vomit in the corner—just
a thimbleful of grey bile. "All this work," I complained, "is fucking with my high. Can't you fig-
ure out some easier way of making a dollar?"

Wayne went to the window. He rapped it several times with his pry bar, each time harder,

until it was loudly destroyed. We threw the stuff out there onto the mud-flattened meadow that came right up below us from the river.

It was quiet in this strange neighborhood along the bank except for the steady breeze in the young leaves. But now we heard a boat coming upstream. The sound curlicued through the riverside saplings like a bee, and in a minute a flat-nosed sports boat cut up the middle of the river going thirty or forty, at least.

This boat was pulling behind itself a tremendous triangular kite on a rope. From the kite, up in the air a hundred feet or so, a woman was suspended, belted in somehow, I would have guessed. She had long red hair. She was delicate and white, and naked except for her beautiful hair. I don't know what she was thinking as she floated past these ruins.

"What's she doing?" was all I could say, though we could see that she was flying.

"Now, that is a beautiful sight," Wayne said.

On the way to town, Wayne asked me to make a long detour onto the Old Highway. He had me pull up to a lopsided farmhouse set on a hill of grass.

"I'm not going in but for two seconds," he said. "You want to come in?"

"Who's here?" I said.

"Come and see," he told me.

It didn't seem anyone was home when we climbed the porch and he knocked. But he didn't knock again, and after a full three minutes a woman opened the door, a slender redhead in a dress printed with small blossoms. She didn't smile. "Hi," was all she said to us.

"Can we come in?" Wayne asked.

"Let me come onto the porch," she said, and walked past us to stand looking out over the fields.

I waited at the other end of the porch, leaning against the rail, and didn't listen. I don't know what they said to one another. She walked down the steps, and Wayne followed. He stood hugging himself and talking down at the earth. The wind lifted and dropped her long red hair. She was about forty, with a bloodless, waterlogged beauty. I guessed Wayne was the storm that had stranded her here.

In a minute he said to me, "Come on." He got in the driver's seat and started the car—you didn't need a key to start it.

I came down the steps and got in beside him.

He looked at her through the windshield. She hadn't gone back inside yet, or done anything at all.

"That's my wife," he told me, as if it wasn't obvious.

I turned around in the seat and studied Wayne's wife as we drove off.

What word can be uttered about those fields? She stood in the middle of them as on a high mountain, with her red hair pulled out sideways by the wind, around her the green and grey plains pressed down flat, and all the grasses of Iowa whistling one note.

I knew who she was.

"That was her, wasn't it?" I said.

Wayne was speechless.

There was no doubt in my mind. She was the woman we'd seen flying over the river. As nearly as I could tell, I'd wandered into some sort of dream that Wayne was having about his wife, and his house. But I didn't say anything more about it.

Because, after all, in small ways, it was turning out to be one of the best days of my life, whether it was somebody else's dream or not. We turned in the scrap wire for twenty-eight dollars—each—at a salvage yard near the gleaming tracks at the edge of town, and went back to the Vine.

Who should be pouring drinks there but a young woman whose name I can't remember. But I remember the way she poured. It was like doubling your money. She wasn't going to make her employers rich. Needless to say, she was revered among us.

"I'm buying," I said.

"No way in hell," Wayne said.

"Come on."

"It is," Wayne said, "my sacrifice."

Sacrifice? Where had he gotten a word like sacrifice? Certainly I had never heard of it.

I'd seen Wayne look across the poker table in a bar and accuse—I do not exaggerate—the biggest, blackest man in Iowa of cheating, accuse him for no other reason than that he, Wayne, was a bit irked by the run of the cards. That was my idea of sacrifice, tossing yourself away, discarding your body. The black man stood up and circled the neck of a beer bottle with his fingers. He was taller than anyone who had ever entered that barroom.

"Step outside," Wayne said.

And the man said, "This ain't school."

"What the goddamn fucking piss-hell," Wayne said, "is that suppose to mean?"

"I ain't stepping outside like you do at school. Make your try right here and now."

"This ain't a place for our kind of business," Wayne said, "not inside here with women and children and dogs and cripples."

"Shit," the man said. "You're just drunk."

"I don't care," Wayne said. "To me you don't make no more noise than a fart in a paper bag."

The huge, murderous man said nothing.

"I'm going to sit down now," Wayne said, "and I'm going to play my game, and fuck you."

The man shook his head. He sat down too. This was an amazing thing. By reaching out one hand and taking hold of it for two or three seconds, he could have popped Wayne's head like an egg.

And then came one of those moments. I remember living through one when I was eighteen and spending the afternoon in bed with my first wife, before we were married. Our naked bodies started glowing, and the air turned such a strange color I thought my life must be leaving me, and with every young fiber and cell I wanted to hold on to it for another breath. A clattering sound was tearing up my head as I staggered upright and opened the door on a vision I will never see again: Where are my women now, with their sweet wet words and ways, and the miraculous balls of hail popping in a green translucence in the yards?

We put on our clothes, she and I, and walked out into a town flooded ankle-deep with white, buoyant stones. Birth should have been like that.

That moment in the bar, after the fight was narrowly averted, was like the green silence after the hailstorm. Somebody was buying a round of drinks. The cards were scattered on the table, face up, face down, and they seemed to foretell that whatever we did to one another would be washed away by liquor or explained away by sad songs.

Wayne was a part of all that.

The Vine was like a railroad club car that had somehow run itself off the tracks into a swamp of time where it awaited the blows of the wrecking ball. And the blows really were coming. Because of Urban Renewal, they were tearing up and throwing away the whole downtown.

And here we were, this afternoon, with nearly thirty dollars each, and our favorite, our very favorite, person tending bar. I wish I could remember her name, but I remember only her grace and her generosity.

All the really good times happened when Wayne was around. But this afternoon, somehow, was the best of all those times. We had money. We were grimy and tired. Usually we felt guilty and frightened, because there was something wrong with us, and we didn't know what it was; but today we had the feeling of men who had worked.

The Vine had no jukebox, but a real stereo continually playing tunes of alcoholic self-pity and sentimental divorce. "Nurse," I sobbed. She poured doubles like an angel, right up to the lip of a cocktail glass, no measuring. "You have a lovely pitching arm." You had to go down to them like a hummingbird over a blossom. I saw her much later, not too many years ago, and when I smiled she seemed to believe I was making advances. But it was only that I remembered. I'll never forget you. Your husband will beat you with an extension cord and the bus will pull away leaving you standing there in tears, but you were my mother.

EMERGENCY

I'd been working in the emergency room for about three weeks, I guess. This was in 1973, before the summer ended. With nothing to do on the overnight shift but batch the insurance reports from the daytime shifts, I just started wandering around, over to the coronary-care unit, down to the cafeteria, et cetera, looking for Georgie, the orderly, a pretty good friend of mine. He often stole pills from the cabinets.

He was running over the tiled floor of the operating room with a mop. "Are you still doing that?" I said.

"Jesus, there's a lot of blood here," he complained.

"Where?" The floor looked clean enough to me.

"What the hell were they doing in here?" he asked me.

"They were performing surgery, Georgie," I told him.

"There's so much goop inside of us, man," he said, "and it all wants to get out." He leaned his mop against a cabinet.

"What are you crying for?" I didn't understand.

He stood still, raised both arms slowly behind his head, and tightened his ponytail. Then he grabbed the mop and started making broad random arcs with it, trembling and weeping and moving all around the place really fast. "What am I *crying* for?" he said. "Jesus. Wow, oh boy, perfect."

I was hanging out in the E.R. with fat, quivering Nurse. One of the Family Service doctors that nobody liked came in looking for Georgie to wipe up after him. "Where's Georgie?" this guy asked.

"Georgie's in O.R.," Nurse said.

"Again?"

"No," Nurse said. "Still."

"Still? Doing what?"

"Cleaning the floor."

"Again?"

"No," Nurse said again. "Still."

Back in O.R., Georgie dropped his mop and bent over in the posture of a child soiling its diapers. He stared down with his mouth open in terror.

He said, "What am I going to do about these fucking *shoes*, man?"

"Whatever you stole," I said, "I guess you already ate it all, right?"

"Listen to how they squish," he said, walking around carefully on his heels.

"Let me check your pockets, man."

He stood still a minute, and I found his stash. I left him two of each, whatever they were. "Shift is about half over," I told him.

"Good. Because I really, really, really need a drink," he said. "Will you please help me get this blood mopped up?"

Around 3:30 a.m. a guy with a knife in his eye came in, led by Georgie.

"I hope *you* didn't do that to him," Nurse said.

"Me?" Georgie said. "No. He was like this."

"My wife did it," the man said. The blade was buried to the hilt in the outside corner of his left eye. It was a hunting knife kind of thing.

"Who brought you in?" Nurse said.

"Nobody. I just walked down. It's only three blocks," the man said.

Nurse peered at him. "We'd better get you lying down."

"Okay, I'm certainly ready for something like that," the man said.

She peered a bit longer into his face.

"Is your other eye," she said, "a glass eye?"

"It's plastic, or something artificial like that," he said.

"And you can see out of *this* eye?" she asked, meaning the wounded one.

"I can see. But I can't make a fist out of my left hand because this knife is doing something to my brain."

"My God," Nurse said.

"I guess I'd better get the doctor," I said.

"There you go," Nurse agreed.

They got him lying down, and Georgie says to the patient, "Name?"

"Terrence Weber."

"Your face is dark. I can't see what you're saying."

"Georgie," I said.

"What are you saying, man? I can't see."

Nurse came over, and Georgie said to her, "His face is dark."

She leaned over the patient. "How long ago did this happen, Terry?" she shouted down into his face.

"Just a while ago. My wife did it. I was asleep," the patient said.

"Do you want the police?"

He thought about it and finally said, "Not unless I die."

Nurse went to the wall intercom and buzzed the doctor on duty, the Family Service person. "Got a surprise for you," she said over the intercom. He took his time getting down the hall to her, because he knew she hated Family Service and her happy tone of voice could only mean something beyond his competence and potentially humiliating.

He peeked into the trauma room and saw the situation: the clerk—that is, me—standing next to the orderly, Georgie, both of us on drugs, looking down at a patient with a knife sticking up out of his face.

"What seems to be the trouble?" he said.

The doctor gathered the three of us around him in the office and said, "Here's the situation. We've got to get a team here, an entire team. I want a good eye man. A great eye man. The best eye man. I want a brain surgeon. And I want a really good gas man, get me a genius. I'm not touching that head. I'm just going to watch this one. I know my limits. We'll just get him prepped and sit tight. Orderly!"

"Do you mean me?" Georgie said. "Should I get him prepped?"

"Is this a hospital?" the doctor asked. "Is this the emergency room? Is that a patient? Are you the orderly?"

I dialled the hospital operator and told her to get me the eye man and the brain man and the gas man.

Georgie could be heard across the hall, washing his hands and singing a Neil Young song that went "Hello, cowgirl in the sand. Is this place at your command?"

"That person is not right, not at all, not one bit," the doctor said.

"As long as my instructions are audible to him it doesn't concern me," Nurse insisted, spooning stuff up out of a little Dixie cup. "I've got my own life and the protection of my family to think of."

"Well, okay, okay. Don't chew my head off," the doctor said.

The eye man was on vacation or something. While the hospital's operator called around to find someone else just as good, the other specialists were hurrying through the night to join us. I stood around looking at charts and chewing up more of Georgie's pills. Some of them tasted the way urine smells, some of them burned, some of them tasted like chalk. Various nurses, and two physicians who'd been tending somebody in I.C.U., were hanging out down here with us now.

Everybody had a different idea about exactly how to approach the problem of removing the knife from Terrence Weber's brain. But when Georgie came in from prepping the patient—from shaving the patient's eyebrow and disinfecting the area around the wound, and so on—he seemed to be holding the hunting knife in his left hand.

The talk just dropped off a cliff.

"Where," the doctor asked finally, "did you get that?"

Nobody said one thing more, not for quite a long time.

After a while, one of the I.C.U. nurses said, "Your shoelace is untied." Georgie laid the knife on a chart and bent down to fix his shoe.

There were twenty more minutes left to get through.

"How's the guy doing?" I asked.

"Who?" Georgie said.

It turned out that Terrence Weber still had excellent vision in the one good eye, and acceptable motor and reflex, despite his earlier motor complaint. "His vitals are normal," Nurse said. "There's nothing wrong with the guy. It's one of those things."

After a while you forget it's summer. You don't remember what the morning is. I'd worked two doubles with eight hours off in between, which I'd spent sleeping on a gurney in the nurse's station. Georgie's pills were making me feel like a giant helium-filled balloon, but I was wide awake. Georgie and I went out to the lot, to his orange pickup.

We lay down on a stretch of dusty plywood in the back of the truck with the daylight knocking against our eyelids and the fragrance of alfalfa thickening on our tongues.

"I want to go to church," Georgie said.

"Let's go to the county fair."

"I'd like to worship. I would."

"They have these injured hawks and eagles there. From the Humane Society," I said.

"I need a quiet chapel about now."

Georgie and I had a terrific time driving around. For a while the day was clear and peaceful. It was one of the moments you stay in, to hell with all the troubles of before and after. The sky is blue and the dead are coming back. Later in the afternoon, with sad resignation, the county fair bares its breasts. A champion of the drug LSD, a very famous guru of the love generation, is being interviewed amid a TV crew off to the left of the poultry cages. His eyeballs look like he bought them in a joke shop. It doesn't occur to me, as I pity this extraterrestrial, that in my life I've taken as much as he has.

After that, we got lost. We drove for hours, literally hours, but we couldn't find the road back to town.

Georgie started to complain. "That was the worst fair I've been to. Where were the rides?"

"They had rides," I said.

"I didn't see one ride."

A jackrabbit scurried out in front of us, and we hit it.

"There was a merry-go-round, a Ferris wheel, and a thing called the Hammer that people were bent over vomiting from after they got off," I said. "Are you completely blind?"

"What was that?"

"A rabbit."

"Something thumped."

"You hit him. *He* thumped."

Georgie stood on the brake pedal. "Rabbit stew."

He threw the truck in reverse and zigzagged back toward the rabbit. "Where's my hunting knife?" He almost ran over the poor animal a second time.

"We'll camp in the wilderness," he said. "In the morning we'll breakfast on its haunches." He was waving Terrence Weber's hunting knife around in what I was sure was a dangerous way.

In a minute he was standing at the edge of the fields, cutting the scrawny little thing up, tossing away its organs. "I should have been a doctor," he cried.

A family in a big Dodge, the only car we'd seen for a long time, slowed down and gawked out the windows as they passed by. The father said, "What is it, a snake?"

"No, it's not a snake," Georgie said. "It's a rabbit with babies inside it."

"Babies!" the mother said, and the father sped

the car forward, over the protests of several little kids in the back.

Georgie came back to my side of the truck with his shirtfront stretched out in front of him as if he were carrying apples in it, or some such, but they were, in fact, slimy miniature bunnies. "No way I'm eating those things," I told him.

"Take them, take them. I gotta drive, take them," he said, dumping them in my lap and getting in on his side of the truck. He started driving along faster and faster, with a look of glory on his face. "We killed the mother and saved the children," he said.

"It's getting late," I said. "Let's get back to town."

"You bet." Sixty, seventy, eighty-five, just topping ninety.

"These rabbits better be kept warm." One at a time I slid the little things in between my shirt buttons and nestled them against my belly. "They're hardly moving," I told Georgie.

"We'll get some milk and sugar and all that, and we'll raise them up ourselves. They'll get as big as gorillas."

The road we were lost on cut straight through the middle of the world. It was still daytime, but the sun had no more power than an ornament or a sponge. In this light the truck's hood, which had been bright orange, had turned a deep blue.

Georgie let us drift to the shoulder of the road, slowly, slowly, as if he'd fallen asleep or given up trying to find his way.

"What is it?"

"We can't go on. I don't have any headlights," Georgie said.

We parked under a strange sky with a faint image of a quarter-moon superimposed on it.

There was a little woods beside us. This day had been dry and hot, the buck pines and what-all simmering patiently, but as we sat there smoking cigarettes it started to get very cold.

"The summer's over," I said.

That was the year when arctic clouds moved down over the Midwest and we had two weeks of winter in September.

"Do you realize it's going to snow?" Georgie asked me.

He was right, a gun-blue storm was shaping up. We got out and walked around idiotically. The beautiful chill! That sudden crispness, and the tang of evergreen stabbing us!

The gusts of snow twisted themselves around our heads while the night fell. I couldn't find the truck. We just kept getting more and more lost.

I kept calling, "Georgie, can you see?" and he kept saying, "See what? See what?"

The only light visible was a streak of sunset flickering below the hem of the clouds. We headed that way.

We bumped softly down a hill toward an open field that seemed to be a military graveyard, filled with rows and rows of austere, identical markers over soldiers' graves. I'd never before come across this cemetery. On the farther side of the field, just beyond the curtains of snow, the sky was torn away and the angels were descending out of a brilliant blue summer, their huge faces streaked with light and full of pity. The sight of them cut through my heart and down the knuckles of my spine, and if there'd been anything in my bowels I would have messed my pants from fear.

Georgie opened his arms and cried out, "It's the drive-in, man!"

"The drive-in . . ." I wasn't sure what these words meant.

"They're showing movies in a fucking blizzard!" Georgie screamed.

"I see. I thought it was something else," I said.

We walked carefully down there and climbed through the busted fence and stood in the very back. The speakers, which I'd mistaken for grave markers, muttered in unison. Then there was tinkly music, of which I could very nearly make out the tune. Famous movie stars rode bicycles beside a river, laughing out of their gigantic, lovely mouths. If anybody had come to see this show, they'd left when the weather started. Not one car remained, not even a broken-down one from last week, or one left here because it was out of gas. In a couple of minutes, in the middle of a whirling square dance, the screen turned black, the cinematic summer ended, the snow went dark, there was nothing but my breath.

"I'm starting to get my eyes back," Georgie said in another minute.

A general greyness was giving birth to various shapes, it was true. "But which ones are close and which ones are far off?" I begged him to tell me.

By trial and error, with a lot of walking back and forth in wet shoes, we found the truck and sat inside it shivering.

"Let's get out of here," I said.

"We can't go anywhere without headlights."

"We've gotta get back. We're a long way from home."

"No, we're not."

"We must have come three hundred miles."

"We're right outside town, Fuckhead. We've just been driving around and around."

"This is no place to camp. I hear the Interstate over there."

"We'll just stay here till it gets late. We can drive home late. We'll be invisible."

We listened to the big rigs going from San Francisco to Pennsylvania along the Interstate, like shudders down a long hacksaw blade, while the snow buried us.

Eventually Georgie said, "We better get some milk for those bunnies."

"We don't have *milk*," I said.

"We'll mix sugar up with it."

"Will you forget about this milk all of a sudden?"

"They're mammals, man."

"Forget about those rabbits."

"Where are they, anyway?"

"You're not listening to me. I said, 'Forget the rabbits.' "

"Where are they?"

The truth was I'd forgotten all about them, and they were dead.

"They slid around behind me and got squashed," I said tearfully.

"They slid around *behind*?"

He watched while I pried them out from behind my back.

I picked them out one at a time and held them in my hands and we looked at them. There were eight. They weren't any bigger than my fingers, but everything was there.

Little feet! Eyelids! Even whiskers! "Deceased," I said.

Georgie asked, "Does everything you touch turn to shit? Does this happen to you every time?"

"No wonder they call me Fuckhead."

"It's a name that's going to stick."

"I realize that."

" 'Fuckhead' is gonna ride you to your grave."

"I just said so. I agreed with you in advance," I said.

Or maybe that wasn't the time it snowed. Maybe it was the time we slept in the truck and I rolled over on the bunnies and flattened them. It doesn't matter. What's important for me to remember now is that early the next morning the snow was melted off the windshield and the daylight woke me up. A mist covered everything and, with the sunshine, was beginning to grow sharp and strange. The bunnies weren't a problem yet, or they'd already been a problem and were already forgotten, and there was nothing on my mind. I felt the beauty of the morning. I could understand how a drowning man might suddenly feel a deep thirst being quenched. Or how the slave might become a friend to his master. Georgie slept with his face right on the steering wheel.

I saw bits of snow resembling an abundance of blossoms on the stems of the drive-in speakers— no, revealing the blossoms that were always there. A bull elk stood still in the pasture beyond the fence, giving off an air of authority and stupidity. And a coyote jogged across the pasture and faded away among the saplings.

That afternoon we got back to work in time to resume everything as if it had never stopped happening and we'd never been anywhere else.

"The Lord," the intercom said, "is my shepherd." It did that each evening because this was a Catholic hospital. "Our Father, who art in Heaven," and so on.

"Yeah, yeah," Nurse said.

The man with the knife in his head, Terrence Weber, was released around suppertime. They'd kept him overnight and given him an eyepatch —all for no reason, really.

He stopped off at E.R. to say goodbye. "Well,

those pills they gave me make everything taste terrible," he said.

"It could have been worse," Nurse said.

"Even my tongue."

"It's just a miracle you didn't end up sightless or at least dead," she reminded him.

The patient recognized me. He acknowledged me with a smile. "I was peeping on the lady next door while she was out there sunbathing," he said. "My wife decided to blind me."

He shook Georgie's hand. Georgie didn't know him. "Who are you supposed to be?" he asked Terrence Weber.

Some hours before that, Georgie had said something that had suddenly and completely explained the difference between us. We'd been driving back toward town, along the Old Highway, through the flatness. We picked up a hitchhiker, a boy I knew. We stopped the truck and the boy climbed slowly up out of the fields as out of the mouth of a volcano. His name was Hardee. He looked even worse than we probably did.

"We got messed up and slept in the truck all night," I told Hardee.

"I had a feeling," Hardee said. "Either that or, you know, driving a thousand miles."

"That too," I said.

"Or you're sick or diseased or something."

"Who's this guy?" Georgie asked.

"This is Hardee. He lived with me last summer. I found him on the doorstep. What happened to your dog?" I asked Hardee.

"He's still down there."

"Yeah, I heard you went to Texas."

"I was working on a bee farm," Hardee said.

"Wow. Do those things sting you?"

"Not like you'd think," Hardee said. "You're part of their daily drill. It's all part of a harmony."

Outside, the same identical stretch of ground repeatedly rolled past our faces. The day was cloudless, blinding. But Georgie said, "Look at that," pointing straight ahead of us.

One star was so hot it showed, bright and blue, in the empty sky.

"I recognized you right away," I told Hardee. "But what happened to your hair? Who chopped it off?"

"I hate to say."

"Don't tell me."

"They drafted me."

"Oh no."

"Oh yeah. I'm AWOL. I'm bad AWOL. I got to get to Canada."

"Oh, that's terrible," I said to Hardee.

"Don't worry," Georgie said. "We'll get you there."

"How?"

"Somehow. I think I know some people. Don't worry. You're on your way to Canada."

That world! These days it's all been erased and they've rolled it up like a scroll and put it away somewhere. Yes, I can touch it with my fingers. But where is it?

After a while Hardee asked Georgie, "What do you do for a job," and Georgie said, "I save lives."

DIRTY WEDDING

I liked to sit up front and ride the fast ones all day long, I liked it when they brushed right up against the buildings north of the Loop and I especially liked it when the buildings dropped away into that bombed-out squalor a little farther north in which people (through windows you'd see a person in his dirty naked kitchen spooning soup toward his face, or twelve children on their bellies on the floor, watching television, but instantly they were gone, wiped away by a movie billboard of a woman winking and touching her upper lip deftly with her tongue, and she in turn erased by a—*wham*, the noise and dark dropped down around your head—tunnel) actually lived.

I was twenty-five, twenty-six, something like that. My fingertips were all yellow from smoking. My girlfriend was with child.

It cost fifty cents, ninety cents, a dollar to ride the train. I really don't remember.

Out in front of the abortion building picketers shook drops of holy water at us and twisted their rosaries around their fingers. A man in dark glasses shadowed Michelle right up the big steps to the door, chanting softly in her ear. I guess he was praying. What were the words of his prayer? I wouldn't mind asking her that question. But it's winter, the mountains around me are tall and deep with snow, and I could never find her now.

Michelle handed her appointment card to the nurse on the third floor. She and the nurse went through a curtain together.

I wandered over across the hall where they were showing a short movie about vasectomies. Much later I told her that I'd actually gotten a vasectomy a long time ago, and somebody else must have made her pregnant. I also told her once that I had inoperable cancer and would soon be passed away and gone, eternally. But nothing I could think up, no matter how dramatic or completely horrible, ever made her repent or love me the way she had at first, before she really knew me.

Anyway they showed the movie to two or three or four of us who were waiting for women across the hall. The scene was cloudy in my sight because I was frightened of whatever they were doing to Michelle and to the other women and of course to the little foetuses. After the film I talked to a man about vasectomies. A man with a mustache. I didn't like him.

"You have to be sure," he said.

"I'm never getting anybody pregnant again. I know that much."

"Would you like to make an appointment?"

"Would you like to give me the money?"

"It won't take long to save the money."

"It would take me forever to save the money," I corrected him.

Then I sat down in the waiting area across the hall. In forty-five minutes the nurse came out and said to me, "Michelle is comfortable now."

"Is she dead?"

"Of course not."

"I kind of wish she was."

She looked frightened. "I don't know what you mean."

I went in through the curtain to see Michelle. She smelled bad.

"How are you feeling?"

"I feel fine."

"What did they stick up you?"

"What?" she said. *"What?"*

The nurse said, "Hey. Out of here. Out of here."

She went through the curtain and came back with a big black guy wearing a starched white shirt and one of those phony gold badges. "I don't think this man needs to be in the building," she said to him, and then she said to me, "Would you like to wait outside, sir?"

"Yeah yeah yeah," I said, and all the way down the big stairs and out the front I said, "Yeah yeah yeah yeah yeah yeah yeah."

It was raining outdoors and most of the Catholics were squashed up under an awning next door with their signs held overhead against the weather. They splashed holy water on my cheek and on the back of my neck, and I didn't feel a thing. Not for many years.

I didn't know what to do now except ride around on the elevated train.

I stepped into one of the cars just as the doors closed; as though the train had waited just for me.

What if there was just snow? Snow everywhere, cold and white, filling every distance? And I just follow my sense of things through this winter until I reach a grove of white trees. And she takes me in.

The wheels screamed, and all I saw suddenly was everybody's big ugly shoes. The sound stopped. We passed solitary, wrenching scenes.

Through the neighborhoods and past the platforms, I felt the cancelled life dreaming after me. Yes, a ghost. A vestige. Something remaining.

At one of the stops down the line there was a problem with the doors. We were delayed, those of us who had destinations, anyway. The train waited and waited in a troubling sleep. Then it hummed softly. You can tell it's going to move before it moves.

A guy stepped in just as the doors closed. The train had waited for him all this time, not a second longer than his arrival, not even half a second, and then it broke the mysterious crystal of its inertia. We'd picked him up and now we were moving. He sat down near the front of the car, completely unaware of his importance. With what kind of miserable or happy fate did he have an appointment across the river?

I decided to follow him.

Several stops later he left the train and went down into a section of squat, repetitive brownstone buildings.

He walked with a bounce, his shoulders looped and his chin scooping forward rhythmically. He didn't look right or left. I supposed he'd walked this route twelve thousand times. He didn't sense or feel me following half a block behind him.

It was a Polish neighborhood somewhere or other. The Polish neighborhoods have that snow. They have that fruit with the light on it, they have that music you can't find. We ended up in a laundromat, where the guy took off his shirt and put it in a washer. He bought some coffee in a paper cup out of a coin machine.

He read the notices on the wall and watched his machine tremble, walking around the place with only his sharkskin sports jacket on. His chest was narrow and white and hair sprouted from around the small nipples.

There were a couple of other men in the laundromat. He chatted with them a little. I could hear one of them say, "The cops wanted to talk to Benny."

"How come? What'd he do?"

"He had a hood up. They were looking for a guy with a hood up."

"What'd he do?"

"Nut'n. Nut'n. Some guy got murdered last night."

And now the man I was following walked right up to me. "You were on the El," he said. He hefted his cup, tossing a sip of coffee between his lips.

I turned away because my throat was closing up. Suddenly I had an erection. I knew men got that way about men, but I didn't know I did. His chest was like Christ's. That's probably who he was.

I could have followed anybody off that train. It would have been the same.

I got back on to ride around some more above the streets.

There was nothing stopping me from going back to where Michelle and I were staying, but these days had reduced us to the Rebel Motel. The maids spat out their chew in the shower stalls. There was a smell of insecticide. I wasn't going back there to sit in the room and wait.

Michelle and I had our drama. It got very dreary sometimes, but it felt like I had to have her. As long as there was one other person at these motels who knew my real name.

Out back they had all these Dumpsters stuffed with God knows what. We can't imagine the shape of our fate, that's for sure.

Think of being curled up and floating in a darkness. Even if you could think, even if you had an imagination, would you ever imagine its opposite, this miraculous world the Asian Taoists call the "Ten Thousand Things"? And if the darkness just got darker? And then you were dead? What would you care? How would you even know the difference?

I sat up front. Right beside me was the little cubicle filled with the driver. You could feel him materializing and dematerializing in there. In the darkness under the universe it didn't matter that the driver was a blind man. He felt the future with his face. And suddenly the train hushed as if the wind had been kicked out of it, and we came into the evening again.

Catty-corner from me sat a dear little black child maybe sixteen, all messed up on skag. She couldn't keep her head up. She couldn't stay out of her dreams. She knew: shit, we might as well have been drinking a dog's tears. Nothing mattered except that we were alive.

"I never tasted black honey," I said to her.

She itched her nose and closed her eyes, her face dipping down into Paradise.

I said, "Hey."

"Black. I ain't black," she said. "I'm yellow. Don't call me black."

"I wish I had some of what you have," I said.

"Gone, boy. Gone, gone, gone." She laughed like God. I didn't blame her for laughing.

"Any chance of getting some more?"

"How much you want? You got ten?"

"Maybe. Sure."

"I'll take you down here," she said. "I'll take you down over to the Savoy." And after two more stops she led me off the train and down into the streets. A few people stood around trashcans with flames leaping up out of them and that sort of thing, mumbling and singing. The streetlamps and traffic lights had wire mesh screens over them.

I know there are people who believe that wherever you look, all you see is yourself. Episodes like this make me wonder if they aren't right.

The Savoy Hotel was a bad place. The reality of it gave out as it rose higher above First Avenue, so that the upper floors dribbled away into space. Monsters were dragging themselves up the stairs. In the basement was a bar going three sides of a rectangle, as big as an Olympic pool, and a dancing stage with a thick gold curtain hanging down over it that never moved. Everyone knew what to do. People were paying with bills they'd made by tearing a corner off a twenty and pasting it onto a one. There was a man with a tall black hat, a helmet of thick blond hair, and a sharp blond beard. He seemed to want to be here. How did he know what to do? Beautiful women in the corners of my sight disappeared when I looked directly at them. Winter outside. Night by afternoon. Darkly, darkly the Happy Hour. I didn't know the rules. I didn't know what to do.

The last time I'd been in the Savoy, it had been in Omaha. I hadn't been anywhere near it in over a year, but I was just getting sicker. When I coughed I saw fireflies.

Everything down there but the curtain was red. It was like a movie of something that was actually happening. Black pimps in fur coats. The women were blank, shining areas with photographs of sad girls floating in them. "I'll just take your money and go upstairs," somebody said to me.

Michelle left me permanently for a man called John Smith, or shall I say that during one of the times we were parted she took up with a man and shortly after that had some bad luck and died? Anyway, she never came back to me.

I knew him, this John Smith. Once at a party he tried to sell me a gun, and later at the same party he made everyone quiet down for a few minutes because I was singing along with the radio, and he liked my voice. Michelle went to Kansas City with him and one night when he was out she took a lot of pills, leaving a note beside her on his pillow where he'd be sure to find it and rescue her. But he was so drunk when he got home that night that he just laid his cheek down on the paper she'd written on, and went to sleep. When he woke up the next morning my beautiful Michelle was cold and dead.

She was a woman, a traitor, and a killer. Males and females wanted her. But I was the only one who ever could have loved her.

For many weeks after she died, John Smith confided to people that Michelle was calling to him from the other side of life. She wooed him. She made herself seem more real than any of the visible people around him, the people who were still breathing, who were supposed to be alive. When I heard, shortly after that, that John Smith was dead, I wasn't surprised.

When we were arguing on my twenty-fourth birthday, she left the kitchen, came back with a pistol, and fired it at me five times from right across the table. But she missed. It wasn't my life she was after. It was more. She wanted to eat my heart and be lost in the desert with what she'd done, she wanted to fall on her knees and give birth from it, she wanted to hurt me as only a child can be hurt by its mother.

I know they argue about whether or not it's right, whether or not the baby is alive at this point or that point in its growth inside the womb. This wasn't about that. It wasn't what the lawyers did. It wasn't what the doctors did, it wasn't what the woman did. It was what the mother and father did together.

THE OTHER MAN

But I never finished telling you about the two men. I never even started describing the second one, whom I met more or less in the middle of Puget Sound, travelling from Bremerton, Washington, to Seattle.

This man was just basically one of those people on a boat, leaning on the rail like the others, his hands dangling over like bait. The day was sunny, unusual for the Northwest Coast. I'm sure we were all feeling blessed on this ferryboat among the humps of very green—in the sunlight almost coolly burning, like phosphorus—islands, and the water of inlets winking in the sincere light of day, under a sky as blue and brainless as the love of God, despite the smell, the slight, dreamy suffocation, of some kind of petroleum-based compound used to seal the deck's seams.

This guy wore horn-rimmed glasses and had a

shy smile, by which I think is generally meant a smile that occurs while the eyes look away.

It was his foreignness, inability to make himself accepted, essential loserness, that made him look away.

"Do you like some beers?"

"Okay," I said.

He bought me a beer and explained that he was from Poland, over here on business. I stayed and talked with him about the obvious things. "It's a beautiful day"—by which we meant that the weather was good. But we never say, "The weather's good," "The weather's pleasant." We say, "It's a beautiful day," "What a beautiful day."

He was a sad case. His jacket was lightweight and yellow. He might have been wearing it for the first time. It was the kind of jacket a foreigner would buy in a store while saying to himself, "I am buying an American jacket." "Are you having," he asked of me, "a family? Any father, mother, brother, sister?"

"I have a brother, one brother, and my parents are both living."

He was driving around in a rented car, with an expense account: a youthful international person doing all right. A certain yearning attached itself between us. I wanted to participate in what was happening to him. It was just a careless, instinctive thing. There was nothing of his I wanted in particular. I wanted it all.

We went downstairs and got in his new-smelling rented car. We waited for the boat to dock and then we drove down the ramp and just a very short ways to a restaurant and tavern on the waterfront, a loud place dappled with sunshine and full of the deep tones of thick beer ware.

I didn't ask him if he had a wife or was father to a family. And he didn't ask me about those things. "Do you ride the motorcycle? I do," he said. "I ride the small, the one, we say, ah, yes, motorscooter, you call it. The big Hell's Angels have the motorcycles, no, I ride the small motorscooter, excuse me. In Warsaw, my city, we drive in the park after twelve in the night, but the rules are saying no, you must not go to the park after this time, 12 p.m. middle-night, yes, ah, midnight, exact, precisely, it's against the rule, the law. It is a law, the park is clawsded. Closed, yes, thank you, it is a law for one months in jail if you try it. Oh, we have a lot fun! I put it on my helmet, and if the polices are catching, they will—bung! bung!—with their sticks! But it doesn't hurt. But we always get away, because they walk, the polices, they have no transportation for that park. We always win! After the middle-night, it is always dark there."

He excused himself and went to find a bathroom and order one more pitcher of beer.

We hadn't yet mentioned our names. We probably wouldn't. In barrooms I lived this over and over.

He came back with the pitcher and poured my glass full and sat down. "Ah hell," he said. "I'm not Polish. I'm from Cleveland."

I was shocked, surprised. Really. Not for one second had I thought of something like this. "Well, tell me some stories about Cleveland, then," I said.

"The Cuyahoga River caught on fire one time," he said. "It was burning in the middle of the night. The fire was just floating along down it. That was interesting to see, because you'd almost expect the fire to stay in the same place, while the water travelled along beneath it. The pollutants caught on fire. Flammable chemicals and waste products from the factories."

"Was any of that stuff you said, was any of it real?"

"The park is real," he said.

"The beer is real," I said.

"And the cops, and the helmet. I really do have

a motorscooter," he said, and assuring me of this seemed to make him feel better.

When I've told others about this man, they've asked me, "Did he make a pass at you?" Yes, he did. But why is that outcome to this encounter obvious to everyone, when it wasn't at all obvious to me, the person who actually met and spoke with him?

Later, when he dropped me off in front of the apartment building where my friends lived, he paused a minute, watching me cross the street, and then left, accelerating swiftly.

I cupped my hands around my mouth like a megaphone. "Maury!" I called, "Carol!" Whenever I came to Seattle, I had to stand out here on the sidewalk and shout up toward their fourth-floor window, because the front entrance was always locked.

"Go away. Get out of here," a lady's voice called from a window on the ground floor, the window of the manager's apartment.

"But my friends live here," I said.

"You can't yell in the streets like that," she said.

She came closer to the window. She had chiselled features, wet eyes, and tendons standing out in her neck. Fanatically religious utterances seemed to quiver on her lips.

"I beg your pardon," I said, "is that a German accent you have there?"

"Don't give me that," she said. "Oh, the lies. You're all so friendly."

"It isn't Polish, I hope."

I stepped back into the street. "Maury!" I screamed. I whistled loudly.

"This is it. That's the finish."

"But they live right up there!"

"I'm going to call the cops. Do you want me to call the cops?"

"Jesus Christ. You bitch," I said.

"I didn't think so. The friendly burglar runs away," she cried after me.

I imagined jamming her into a roaring fireplace. The screams. . . . Her face caught fire and burned.

The sky was a bruised red shot with black, almost exactly the colors of a tattoo. Sunset had two minutes left to live.

The street I stood on rolled down a long hill toward First and Second Avenue, the lowest part of town. My feet carried me away down the hill. I danced on my despair. I trembled outside a tavern called Kelly's, nothing but a joint, its insides swimming in a cheesy light. Peeking inside I thought, If I have to go in there and drink with those old men.

Right across the street was a hospital. In a radius of only a few blocks, there were four or five. Two men in pajamas stood looking out a window of this one, on the third floor. One of the men was talking. I could almost trace their steps back to the rooms from which they'd wandered tonight with everything they stood for disrupted by their maladies.

Two people, two hospital patients up out of their beds after supper, find each other wandering the halls, and they stand for a while in a little lounge that smells of cigarette butts, looking out over the parking lot. These two, this man and this man, they don't have their health. Their solitudes are fearful. And then they find one another.

But do you think one is ever going to visit the other one's grave?

I pushed through the door into Kelly's. Inside they sat with their fat hands around their beers while the jukebox sang softly to itself. You'd think they'd found out how, by sitting still and holding their necks just so, to look down into lost worlds.

There was one woman in the place. She was drunker than I was. We danced, and she told me she was in the army.

"I'm locked out of my friends'," I told her.

"Don't worry about a thing like that," she said, and kissed my cheek.

I held her close. She was short, just the right size for me. I drew her closer.

Among the men around us, somebody cleared his throat. The bass's rhythm travelled the floor-boards, but I doubt it reached them.

"Let me kiss you," I pleaded. Her lips tasted cheap. "Let me go home with you," I said. She kissed me sweetly.

She'd outlined her eyes in black. I loved her eyes. "My husband's at home," she said. "We can't go there."

"Maybe we could get a motel room."

"It depends on how much money you have."

"Not enough. Not enough," I admitted.

"I'll have to take you home."

She kissed me.

"What about your husband?"

She just kept kissing me as we danced. There was nothing in the world for these men to do but watch, or look at their drinks. I don't remember what was playing, but in that era in Seattle the much favored sad jukebox song was called "Misty Blue"; probably "Misty Blue" was playing as I held her and felt her ribs moving in my hands.

"I can't let you get away," I told her.

"I could take you home. You could sleep on the couch. Then later on I could come out."

"While your husband's in the next room?"

"He'll be asleep. I could say you're my cousin."

We pressed ourselves together gently and furiously. "I want to love you, baby," she said.

"Oh, God. But I don't know, with your husband there."

"Love me," she begged. She wept onto my chest.

"How long have you been married?" I asked.

"Since Friday."

"Friday?"

"They gave me four days' leave."

"You mean the day before yesterday was your wedding day?"

"I could tell him you're my brother," she suggested.

First I put my lips to her upper lip, then to the bottom of her pout, and then I kissed her fully, my mouth on her open mouth, and we met inside.

It was there. It was. The long walk down the hall. The door opening. The beautiful stranger. The torn moon mended. Our fingers touching away the tears. It was there.

HAPPY HOUR

I was after a seventeen-year-old belly dancer who was always in the company of a boy who claimed to be her brother, but he wasn't her brother, he was just somebody who was in love with her, and she let him hang around because life can be that way.

I was in love with her, too. But she was still in love with a man who'd recently gone to prison.

I looked in all the worst locations, the Vietnam Bar and so on.

The bartender said, "Do you want a drink?"

"He doesn't have money to drink."

I did, but not enough to drink for the whole two hours.

I tried inside the Jimjam Club. Indians from Klamath or Kootenai or up higher—British Columbia, Saskatchewan—sat in a row along the bar like little icons, or fat little dolls, things mistreated at the hands of a child. She wasn't there.

A guy, a slit-eyed, black-eyed Nez Perce, nearly elbowed me off the stool as he leaned over ordering a glass of the least expensive port wine. I said, "Hey, wasn't I shooting pool in here with you yesterday?"

"No, I don't think so."

"And you said if I'd rack you'd get change in a minute and pay me back?"

"I wasn't here yesterday. I wasn't in town."

"And then you never paid me the quarter? You owe me a quarter, man."

"I gave you that quarter. I put the quarter right by your hand. Two dimes and a nickel."

"Somebody's gonna get fucked up over this."

"Not me. I paid you that quarter. Probably it fell on the floor."

"Do you know when that's *it?* Do you know when it's the end?"

"Eddie, Eddie," the Indian said to the bartender, "did you find any dimes and nickels down here on the floor yesterday? Did you sweep up? Did you sweep anything like that, maybe two dimes and a nickel?"

"Probably. I usually do. Who cares?"

"See?" the guy said to me.

"You make me so tired," I said, "I can hardly move my fingers. All of you."

"Hey, I wouldn't fuck you around over a quarter."

"All of you, every last one."

"Do you want a quarter? It's bullshit. Here."

"Fuck it. Just die," I said, pushing off.

"Take the quarter," he said, very loudly, now that he could see I wouldn't touch it.

Just the night before, she'd let me sleep in the same bed, not exactly with her, but beside her. She was staying with three college girls of whom two had Taiwanese boyfriends. Her fake brother slept on the floor. When we woke up in the morning he didn't say anything. He never did—it was the secret of his success, such as it was. I gave four dollars, almost all my money, to one of the college girls and her boyfriend, who didn't speak English. They were going to get us all some Taiwanese pot. I stood at the window looking at the apartment building's parking lot while the brother brushed his teeth, and watched them leave with my money in a green sedan. They ran into a phone pole before they were even out of the parking lot. They got out of the sedan and staggered away, leaving the car doors open, clinging to each other, their hair flying around their faces in the wind.

I was sitting on the city bus—this was in Seattle—later that morning. I was down front, in the long seat that faces sideways. A woman across from me held a large English-literature textbook in her lap. Next to her sat a light-skinned black man. "Yeah," she said to him. "Today's payday. And it feels good, even if it's not gonna last." He looked at her. His big forehead made him seem thoughtful. "Well," he said, "I got twenty-four hours left in this town."

The weather outside was clear and calm. Most days in Seattle are grey, but now I remember only the sunny ones.

I rode around on the bus for three or four hours. By then a huge Jamaican woman was steering the thing. "You can't just sit on the bus," she said, talking to me in her rearview mirror. "You've got to have a destination."

"I'll get off at the library, then," I said.

"That'll be fine."

"I know it'll be fine," I told her.

I stayed in the library, crushed breathless by the smoldering power of all those words—many of them unfathomable—until Happy Hour. And then I left.

The motor traffic was relentless, the sidewalks

were crowded, the people were preoccupied and mean, because Happy Hour was also Rush Hour.

During Happy Hour, when you pay for one drink, he gives you two.

Happy Hour lasts two hours.

All this time I kept my eye out for the belly dancer. Her name was Angelique. I wanted to find her because, despite her other involvements, she seemed to like me. I'd liked her the minute I'd seen her the first time. She was resting at a table between numbers in the Greek nightclub where she was dancing. A little of the stage light touched her. She was very frail. She seemed to be thinking about something far away, waiting patiently for somebody to destroy her. One of the other dancers, a chop-haired, mannish sort of person, stayed close to her and said, "What do you think you want, boyo?" to a sailor who offered to buy her a drink. Angelique herself said nothing. This virginal sadness wasn't all fake. There was a part of her she hadn't yet allowed to be born because it was too beautiful for this place, that was true. But she was mostly a torn-up trollop. "Just trying to get over," the sailor said. "The way they charge for these drinks, you think you'd be half-complimented." "She doesn't need your compliments," the older dancer said. "She's tired."

By now it was six. I walked over and stopped in at the Greek place. But they told me she'd left town.

The day was ending in a fiery and glorious way. The ships on the Sound looked like paper silhouettes being sucked up into the sun.

I had two doubles and immediately it was as if I'd been dead forever, and was now finally awake.

I was in Pig Alley. It was directly on the harbor, built out over the waters on a rickety pier, with floors of carpeted plywood and a Formica bar. The cigarette smoke looked unearthly. The sun lowered itself through the roof of clouds, ignited the sea, and filled the big picture window with molten light, so that we did our dealing and dreaming in a brilliant fog. People entering the bars on First Avenue gave up their bodies. Then only the demons inhabiting us could be seen. Souls who had wronged each other were brought together here. The rapist met his victim, the jilted child discovered its mother. But nothing could be healed, the mirror was a knife dividing everything from itself, tears of false fellowship dripped on the bar. And what are you going to do to me now? With what, exactly, would you expect to frighten me?

Something embarrassing had happened in the library. An older gentleman had come over from the checkout counter with his books in his arms and addressed me softly, in the tones of a girl. "Your zipper," he said, "is open. I thought I'd better tell you."

"Okay," I said. I reached down quickly and zipped my fly.

"Quite a few people were noticing," he said.

"Okay. Thanks."

"You're welcome," he said.

I could have gotten him around the neck right then, right there in the library, and killed him. Stranger things have happened on this earth. But he turned away.

Pig Alley was a cheap place. I sat next to a uniformed nurse with a black eye.

I recognized her. "Where's your boyfriend today?"

"Who?" she said innocently.

"I gave him ten dollars and he disappeared."

"When?"

"Last week."

"I haven't seen him."

"He should be more grown up."

"He's probably in Tacoma."

"How old is he, about thirty?"

"He'll be back tomorrow."

"He's too old to be yanking people off for a dime."

"Do you want to buy a pill? I need the money."

"What kind of pill?"

"It's psychedelic mushrooms all ground up."

She showed me. Nobody could have swallowed that thing.

"That's the biggest pill I've ever seen."

"I'll sell it for three dollars."

"I didn't know they made capsules that size. What size is that? Number One?"

"It's a Number One, yeah."

"Look at it! It's like an egg. It's like an Easter thing."

"Wait," she said, looking at my money. "No, right, yeah—three dollars. Some days I can't even count!"

"Here goes."

"Just keep drinking. Wash it down. Drink the whole beer."

"Wow. How did I do that? Sometimes I think I'm not human."

"Would you have another dollar? This one's kind of wrinkly."

"I never swallowed a Number One before."

"It's a big cap, for sure."

"The biggest there is. Is it for horses?"

"No."

"It's gotta be for horses."

"No. For horses they squirt a paste in its mouth," she explained. "The paste is so sticky the horse can't spit it out. They don't make horse pills anymore."

"They don't?"

"Not anymore."

"But if they did," I said.

STEADY HANDS
AT SEATTLE GENERAL

Inside of two days I was shaving myself, and I even shaved a couple of new arrivals, because the drugs they injected me with had an amazing effect. I call it amazing because only hours before they'd wheeled me through corridors in which I hallucinated a soft, summery rain. In the hospital rooms on either side, objects—vases, ashtrays, beds—had looked wet and scary, hardly bothering to cover up their true meanings.

They ran a few syringesful into me, and I felt like I'd turned from a light, Styrofoam thing into a person. I held up my hands before my eyes. The hands were as still as a sculpture's.

I shaved my roommate, Bill. "Don't get tricky with my mustache," he said.

"Okay so far?"

"So far."

"I'll do the other side."

"That would make sense, partner."

Just below one cheekbone, Bill had a small blemish where a bullet had entered his face, and in the other cheek a slightly larger scar where the slug had gone on its way.

"When you were shot right through your face like that, did the bullet go on to do anything interesting?"

"How would I know? I didn't take notes. Even if it goes on through, you still feel like you just got shot in the head."

"What about this little scar here, through your sideburn?"

"I don't know. Maybe I was born with that one. I never saw it before."

"Someday people are going to read about you in a story or a poem. Will you describe yourself for those people?"

"Oh, I don't know. I'm a fat piece of shit, I guess."

"No. I'm serious."

"You're not going to write about me."

"Hey. I'm a writer."

"Well then, just tell them I'm overweight."

"He's overweight."

"I been shot twice."

"Twice?"

"Once by each wife, for a total of three bullets, making four holes, three ins and one out."

"And you're still alive."

"Are you going to change any of this for your poem?"

"No. It's going in word for word."

"That's too bad, because asking me if I'm alive makes you look kind of stupid. Obviously, I am."

"Well, maybe I mean alive in a deeper sense. You could be talking, and still not be alive in a deeper sense."

"It don't get no deeper than the kind of shit we're in right now."

"What do you mean? It's great here. They even give you cigarettes."

"I didn't get any yet."

"Here you go."

"Hey. Thanks."

"Pay me back when they give you yours."

"Maybe."

"What did you say when she shot you?"

"I said, 'You shot me!' "

"Both times? Both wives?"

"The first time I didn't say anything, because she shot me in the mouth."

"So you couldn't talk."

"I was knocked out cold, is the reason I couldn't talk. And I still remember the dream I had while I was knocked out that time."

"What was the dream?"

"How could I tell you about it? It was a dream. It didn't make any fucking sense, man. But I do remember it."

"You can't describe it even a little bit?"

"I really don't know what the description would be. I'm sorry."

"Anything. Anything at all."

"Well, for one thing, the dream is something that keeps coming back over and over. I mean, when I'm awake. Every time I remember my first wife, I remember that she pulled the trigger on me, and then, here comes that dream . . .

"And the dream wasn't—there wasn't anything sad about it. But when I remember it, I get like, *Fuck, man, she really, she shot me. And here's that dream.*"

"Did you ever see that Elvis Presley movie, *Follow That Dream?*"

"*Follow That Dream.* Yeah, I did. I was just going to mention that."

"Okay. You're all done. Look in the mirror."

"Right."

"What do you see?"

"How did I get so fat, when I never eat?"

"Is that all?"

"Well, I don't know. I just got here."

"What about your life?"

"Hah! That's a good one."

"What about your past?"

"What about it?"

"When you look back, what do you see?"

"Wrecked cars."

"Any people in them?"

"Yes."

"Who?"

"People who are just meat now, man."

"Is that really how it is?"

"How do I know how it is? I just got here. And it stinks."

"Are you kidding? They're pumping Haldol by the quart. It's a playpen."

"I hope so. Because I been in places where all they do is wrap you in a wet sheet, and let you bite down on a little rubber toy for puppies."

"I could see living here two weeks out of every month."

"Well, I'm older than you are. You can take a couple more rides on this wheel and still get out with all your arms and legs stuck on right. Not me."

"Hey. You're doing fine."

"Talk into here."

"Talk into your bullet hole?"

"Talk into my bullet hole. Tell me I'm fine."

BEVERLY HOME

Sometimes I went during my lunch break into a big nursery across the street, a glass building full of plants and wet earth and feeling of cool dead sex. During this hour the same woman always watered the dark beds with a hose. Once I talked with her, mostly about myself and about, stupidly, my problems. I asked her for her number. She said she had no phone, and I got the feeling she was purposely hiding her left hand, maybe because she wore a wedding ring. She wanted me to come by and see her again sometime. But I left knowing I wouldn't go back. She seemed much too grown-up for me.

And sometimes a dust storm would stand off in the desert, towering so high it was like another

city—a terrifying new era approaching, blurring
our dreams.

I was a whimpering dog inside, nothing more
than that. I looked for work because people
seemed to believe I should look for work, and
when I found a job I believed I was happy about
it because these same people—counselors and
Narcotics Anonymous members and such—
seemed to think a job was a happy thing.

Maybe, when you hear the name "Beverly,"
you think of Beverly Hills—people wandering the
streets with their heads shot off by money.

As for me, I don't remember ever knowing anybody named Beverly. But it's a beautiful, a son-
orous name. I worked in an O-shaped, turquoise-
blue hospital for the aged bearing it.

Not all the people living at Beverly Home were
old and helpless. Some were young but paralyzed. Some weren't past middle age but were
already demented. Others were fine, except that
they couldn't be allowed out on the street with
their impossible deformities. They made God

look like a senseless maniac. One man had a con-
genital bone ailment that had turned him into a
seven-foot-tall monster. His name was Robert.
Each day Robert dressed himself in a fine suit,
or a blazer-and-trousers combination. His hands
were eighteen inches long. His head was like a
fifty-pound Brazil nut with a face. You and I
don't know about these diseases until we get
them, in which case we also will be put out of
sight.

This was part-time work. I was responsible for
the facility's newsletter, just a few mimeographed
pages issued twice a month. Also it was part of
my job to touch people. The patients had nothing
to do but stumble or wheel themselves through
the wide halls in a herd. Traffic flowed in one
direction only, those were the rules. I walked
against the tide, according to my instructions,
greeting everybody and grasping their hands or
squeezing their shoulders, because they needed
to be touched, and they didn't get much of that.
I always said hello to a grey-haired man in his
early forties, vigorous and muscular, but completely senile. He'd take me by the shirtfront and
say things like, "There's a price to be paid for
dreaming." I covered his fingers with my own.
Nearby was a woman nearly falling out of her
wheelchair and hollering, "Lord? Lord?" Her

feet pointed left, her head looked to the right, and her arms twisted around her like ribbons around a Maypole. I put my hands in her hair. Meanwhile around us ambled all these people whose eyes made me think of clouds and whose bodies made me think of pillows. And there were others out of whom all the meat appeared to have been sucked by the strange machines they kept in the closets around here—hygienic things. Most of these people were far enough gone that they couldn't bathe themselves. They had to be given their baths by professionals using shiny hoses with sophisticated nozzles.

There was a guy with something like multiple sclerosis. A perpetual spasm forced him to perch sideways on his wheelchair and peer down along his nose at his knotted fingers. This condition had descended on him suddenly. He got no visitors. His wife was divorcing him. He was only thirty-three, I believe he said, but it was hard to guess what he told about himself because he really couldn't talk anymore, beyond clamping his lips repeatedly around his protruding tongue while groaning.

No more pretending for him! He was completely and openly a mess. Meanwhile the rest of us go on trying to fool each other.

I always looked in on a man named Frank,

amputated above both knees, who greeted me with a magisterial sadness and a nod at his empty pajama-pants legs. All day long he watched television from his bed. It wasn't his physical condition that kept him here, but his sadness.

The home lay in a cul-de-sac in east Phoenix, with a view into the desert surrounding the city. This was in the spring of that year, the season when some varieties of cactus produced tiny blossoms out of their thorns. To catch the bus home each day I walked through a vacant lot, and sometimes I'd run right up on one—one small orange flower that looked as if it had fallen down here from Andromeda, surrounded by a part of the world cast mainly in eleven hundred shades of brown, under a sky whose blueness seemed to get lost in its own distances. Dizzy, enchanted— I'd have felt the same if I'd been walking along and run into an elf out here sitting in a little chair. The desert days were already burning, but nothing could stifle these flowers.

One day, too, when I'd passed through the lot and was walking along behind a row of town houses on the way to the bus stop, I heard the sound of a woman singing in her shower. I thought of mermaids: the blurry music of falling water, the soft song from the wet chamber. The dusk was down, and the heat came off the hov-

ering buildings. It was rush hour, but the desert
sky has a way of absorbing the sounds of traffic
and making them seem idle and small. Her voice
was the clearest thing coming to my ears.

She sang with the unconsciousness, the obliv-
iousness, of a castaway. She must not have understood that somebody might be able to hear her.
It sounded like an Irish hymn.

I thought I might be tall enough to peek inside
her window, and it didn't look like anybody
would catch me at it.

These town houses went in for that desert
landscaping—gravel and cactus instead of a
lawn. I had to walk softly so as not to crunch—
not that anybody would have heard my steps.
But I didn't want to hear them myself.

Under the window I was camouflaged by a trel-
lis and a vine of morning glories. The traffic went
by as always; nobody noticed me. It was one of
those small, high bathroom windows. I had to
stand on tiptoe and grip the windowsill to keep
my chin above it. She'd already stepped from the
shower, a woman as soft and young as her voice,
but not a girl. Her physique was on the chunky
side. She had light hair falling straight and wet
almost to the small of her back. She faced away.
Mist covered her mirror, and also the window,
just a bit; otherwise she might have seen my eyes

reflected there from behind her. I felt weightless.
I had no trouble clinging to the windowsill. I knew
that if I let go I wouldn't have the gall to raise
my face back up again—by then she might have
turned toward the window, might give a yell.

She towelled off quickly, briskly, never touching herself in any indulgent or particularly sen-
sual way. That was disappointing. But it was
virginal and exciting, too. I had thoughts of
breaking through the glass and raping her. But
I would have been ashamed to have her see me.
I thought I might be able to do something like
that if I were wearing a mask.

My bus went by. Bus 24—it didn't even slow
down. Just a glimpse, but I could see how tired
everybody inside it must have been, simply by
the way they held themselves, pitching to and fro.
Many of them I vaguely recognized. Usually we
all rode together back and forth, work and home,
home and work, but not tonight.

It wasn't all that dark yet. The cars, however,
were fewer now; most of the commuters were already in their living rooms watching TV. But not
her husband. He drove up while I was there by
his bathroom window trying to peek at his wife.
I had a feeling, a terrible touch against my neck,
and ducked beside a cactus just before his car
turned into the drive, at which point his eyes

would have swept the wall where I was standing.
The car turned into the driveway, out of sight
around the building's other side, and I heard the
engine die and its last sounds echo out over the
evening.

His wife had finished her bath. The door was
just shutting behind her. There seemed to be
nothing left in that bathroom then but the flatness
of that door.

Now that she'd left the bathroom she was lost
to me. I wouldn't be able to peek at her because
the other windows lay around the building's corner and were visible, full on, from the street.

I got out of there and waited forty-five minutes
for the next bus, the last one on the schedule.
By then it was pretty well dark. On the bus I sat
in the strange, artificial light with my notebook
in my lap, working on my newsletter. "We've got
a new crafts hour, too"—I wrote in a bumpy
scrawl—"Mondays at 2:00 p.m. Our last project
was making animals out of dough. Grace Wright
made a dandy Snoopy dog and Clarence Lovell
made a gunboat. Others made miniature ponds,
turtles, frogs, ladybugs, and more."

The first woman I actually dated during this
era was somebody I met at a "Sober Dance," a

social event for recovering drunkards and dope addicts, people like me. She didn't have such problems herself, but her husband had, and he'd run off somewhere long ago. Now she put in time here and there as a volunteer for charity, though she worked a full-time job and was raising a little daughter. We started dating regularly, every Saturday night, and we slept together, too, at her apartment, though I never stayed all the way through to breakfast.

This woman was quite short, well under five feet, closer, in fact, to four and half feet tall. Her arms weren't proportional to her body, or at least not to her torso, although they matched her legs, which were also exceptionally abbreviated. Medically speaking, she was a dwarf. But that wasn't the first thing you noticed about her. She had large, Mediterranean eyes, full of a certain amount of smoke and mystery and bad luck. She'd learned how to dress so you didn't observe right away that she was a dwarf. When we made love, we were the same size, because her torso was ordinary. It was only her arms and legs that had come out too short. We made love on the floor in her TV room after she got her little daughter down for the night. Between our jobs and her routines with the little girl, we were kept to a kind of schedule. The same shows were always playing when we made love. They were stupid shows, Saturday-night shows. But I was afraid to make love to her without the conversations and laughter from that false universe playing in our ears, because I didn't want to get to know her very well, and didn't want to be bridging any silences with our eyes.

Usually before that we'd have gone to dinner at one of the Mexican places—the posh ones, with the adobe walls and the velvet paintings that would have been cheap in anybody's home—and we'd have filled each other in on the week's happenings. I told her all about my job at Beverly Home. I was taking a new approach to life. I was trying to fit in at work. I wasn't stealing. I was trying to see each task through to the end. That kind of thing. She, for her part, worked at an airline ticket counter, and I suppose she stood on a box to accomplish her transactions. She had an understanding soul. I had no trouble presenting myself to her pretty much as I actually was, except when it came to one thing.

The spring was on and the days were getting longer. I missed my bus often, waiting to spy on the wife in the town-house apartment.

How could I do it, how could a person go that low? And I understand your question, to which I reply, Are you kidding? That's nothing. I'd been much lower than that. And I expected to see myself do worse.

Stopping there and watching while she showered, watching her step out naked, dry off, and leave the bathroom, and then listening to the sounds her husband made coming home in his car and walking through the front door, all of this became a regular part of my routine. They did the same thing every day. On the weekends I don't know, because I didn't work then. I don't think the weekend buses ran on the same schedule anyway.

Sometimes I saw her and sometimes I didn't. She never did anything she might have been embarrassed about, and I didn't learn any of her secrets, though I wanted to, especially because she didn't know me. She probably couldn't even have imagined me.

Usually her husband came home before I left, but he didn't cross my line of sight. One day I went to their house later than usual, went to the front instead of around to the back. This time I walked past the house just as her husband was getting out of his car. There wasn't much to see, just a man coming home to his supper like anybody else. I'd been curious, and now that I'd had a look at him I could be sure I didn't like him. His head was bald on top. His suit was baggy, wrinkled, comical. He wore a beard, but he shaved his upper lip.

I didn't think he belonged with his wife. He was middle-aged or better. She was young. I was young. I imagined running away with her. Cruel giants, mermaids, captivating spells, a hunger for such things seemed to want to play itself out within the desert springtime and its ambushes, its perfumes.

I watched him go inside, then I waited up at my bus stop till it was night. I didn't care about the bus. I was waiting for darkness, when I could stand out front of their house without being seen and look right into their living room.

Through the front window I watched them eat supper. She was dressed in a long skirt and wore a white cloth over the crown of her head, something like a skullcap. Before they ate, they dipped their faces and prayed for three or four full minutes.

It had struck me that the husband looked very

somber, very old-fashioned, with his dark suit and big shoes, his Lincoln beard and shiny head. Now that I saw the wife in the same kind of getup, I understood: they were Amish, or more likely Mennonites. I knew the Mennonites did missionary work overseas, works of lonely charity in strange worlds where nobody spoke their language. But I wouldn't have expected to find a couple of them all alone in Phoenix, living in an apartment, because these sects normally kept to the rural areas. There was a Bible college nearby; they must have come to take some courses there.

I was excited. I wanted to watch them fucking. I wondered how I could manage to be here when that was happening. If I came back one night late, after dark, I'd be able to stand by the bedroom window without being seen from the street. The idea made me dizzy. I was sick of myself and full of joy. Just watching for a glimpse of her as she stepped from the shower didn't seem enough anymore, and I left and went back and waited to get on bus 24. But it was too late, because the last bus had already gone by.

On Thursdays at Beverly Home the oldest patients were rounded up and placed in chairs in the cafeteria before paper cups of milk and given paper plates with cookies on them. They played a game called "I Remember"—a thing to keep them involved with the details of their lives before they slipped away into senility beyond anybody's reach. Each one would talk about what had happened that morning, what had happened last week, what had happened in the past few minutes.

Once in a while they had a little party, with cupcakes, honoring yet one more year in somebody's life. I had a list of dates, and kept everybody informed:

"And on the tenth, Isaac Christopherson turned a whopping ninety-seven! Many happy returns! There'll be six birthday people next month. Watch for April's *Beverly Home News* to find out who they are!"

The rooms were set off a hallway that curved until it circled back on itself completely and you found the room you'd first looked in on. Sometimes it seemed to curve back around in a narrowing spiral, shrinking toward the heart of it all, which was the room you'd begun with—any of the rooms, the room with the man who kept his stumps cuddled like pets under the comforter or the room with the woman who cried, "Lord? Lord?" or the room with the man with blue skin or the room with the man and wife who no longer remembered each other's name.

I didn't spend a lot of time here—ten, twelve hours a week, something like that. There were other things to do. I looked for a real job, I went to a therapy group for heroin addicts, I reported regularly to the local Alcoholic Reception Center, I took walks in the desert springtime. But I felt about the circular hallway of Beverly Home as about the place where, between our lives on this earth, we go back to mingle with other souls waiting to be born.

Thursday nights I usually went to an AA meeting in an Episcopal church's basement. We sat around collapsible tables looking very much like people stuck in a swamp—slapping at invisible things, shifting, squirming, scratching, rubbing the flesh of our arms and our necks. "I used to walk around in the night," one guy said, a guy named Chris—kind of a friend, we'd been in Detox together—"all alone, all screwed-up. Did you ever walk around like that past the houses with their curtains in the windows, and you feel like you're dragging a cart of sins behind you, and did you ever think: Behind those windows, behind those curtains, people are leading normal, happy lives?" This was just rhetorical, just part of what he said when it was his turn to say something.

But I got up and left the room and stood around outside the church, smoking lousy low-tar cigarettes, my guts jumping with unintelligible words, until the meeting broke up and I could beg a lift back to my neighborhood.

As for the Mennonite couple, you could almost say that our schedules were coordinated now. I spent a lot of time outside their building, after sundown, in the rapidly cooling dark. Any window suited me by this time. I just wanted to see them at home together.

She always wore a long skirt, flat-heeled walking shoes or sneakers, delicate white socks. She kept her hair pinned up and covered with a white skullcap. Her hair, when it wasn't wet, was quite blond.

I got so I enjoyed seeing them sitting in their living room talking, almost not talking at all, reading the Bible, saying grace, eating their supper in the kitchen alcove, as much as I liked watching her naked in the shower.

If I wanted to wait till it was dark enough, I

could stand by the bedroom window without
being seen from the street. Several nights I stayed
there until they fell asleep. But they never made
love. They lay there and never even touched each
other, as far as I knew. My guess was that in that
kind of religious community they were kept to a
schedule or something. How often were they allowed to have each other? Once a month? Or once
a year? Or for the purpose, only, of getting children? I started to wonder if maybe the morning
was their time, if maybe I should come in the
morning. But then it would be too light. I was
anxious to catch them at it soon, because now-
adays they slept with the windows open and the
curtains slightly parted. Before much longer it
would be too hot for that; they'd turn on the
central cooling and shut themselves away.

After a month, or very nearly, the particular
night came when I heard her crying out. They'd
left the living room just minutes before. It hardly
seemed they'd had time to get undressed. They'd
put away the things they were reading a little
while before that and had been talking quietly,
he lying back on the couch and she sitting in the
easy chair perpendicular to it. There'd been
nothing of the lover about him right then. He
hadn't seemed inflamed, but maybe a little ner-
vous, touching the edge of the coffee table with

an idle hand and rocking it while they talked.

Now they weren't talking, though. It was almost as if she were singing, as I'd heard her do
many times when she thought she was by herself.
I hurried around from the living-room window
to the bedroom.

They'd closed the bedroom window, and the
curtains, too. I couldn't hear what they were saying, but I heard the bedsprings, I was sure of
that, and her lovely cries. And soon he was shout-
ing also, like a preacher on the stump. Meanwhile
I was lurking there in the dark, trembling, really,
from the pit of my stomach out to my fingertips.
Two inches of crack at the curtain's edge, that's
all I could have, all I could have, it seemed, in
the whole world. I could have one corner of the
bed, and shadows moving in a thin band of light
from the living room. I felt wronged—it wasn't
that hot tonight, other people had their windows
open, I heard voices, music, messages from their
televisions, and their cars going by and their
sprinklers hissing. But of the Mennonites, almost
nothing. I felt abandoned—cast out of the fold.
I was ready to break the glass with a rock.

But already their cries were over. I tried the
window's other end, where the curtains were
drawn more snugly, and though the view was
narrower, the angle was better. From this side I

could see shadows moving in the light from the living room. In fact, they'd never made it to the bed. They were standing upright. Not passionately twining. More likely they were fighting. The bedroom lamp came on. Then a hand drew the curtain aside. Just like that I was staring into her face.

I thought to run, but it was such a nauseating jolt that suddenly I didn't know how to move. But after all it didn't matter. My face wasn't two feet from hers, but it was dark out and she could only have been looking at her own reflection, not at me. She was alone in the bedroom. She still had all her clothes on. I had the same flutter in my heart that I got when I happened to stroll past a car parked off by itself somewhere, with a guitar or a suede jacket on the front seat, and I'd think: But anybody could steal this.

I stood on the dark side of her and actually couldn't see very well, but I got the impression she was upset. I thought I heard her weeping. I could have touched a teardrop, I stood that close. I was pretty sure that, shadowed as I was, she wouldn't notice me now, unless perhaps I made a movement, so I stayed very still while absently she put her hand to her head and removed the little bonnet, the skullcap. I peered at her dark face until I was sure she was grieving—chewing her lower lip, staring, and letting the tears fall across her cheeks.

In just a minute or so, her husband came back. He took several steps into the room and paused like somebody, a boxer or a football player maybe, trying to walk with an injury. They'd been arguing, and he was sorry; it was plain in the way he stood there with his jaw stuck on a word and kind of holding his apology in his hands. But his wife wouldn't turn around.

He put an end to the argument by getting down before her and washing her feet.

First he left the room once more, and after a while he returned with a basin, a yellow plastic thing for washing the dishes, carrying it in a careful way that made it obvious there was water sloshing inside it. He had a kitchen towel draped over one shoulder. He put the basin on the floor and went down on one knee, head bowed, as if he were proposing to her. She didn't move for a while, not perhaps for a full minute, which seemed like a very long time to me outside in the dark with a great loneliness and the terror of a whole life not yet lived, and the TVs and garden sprinklers making the noises of a thousand lives never to be lived, and the cars going by with the sound of passage, movement, untouchable, uncatchable. Then she turned toward him, slipped her tennis shoes from her feet, reached backward to each lifted ankle one after the other, and peeled the small white socks off. She dipped the toe of her right foot into the water, then the whole foot, lowering it down out of sight into the yellow basin. He took the cloth from his shoulder, never once looking up at her, and started the washing.

By this time I wasn't dating the Mediterranean beauty anymore; I was seeing another woman, who was of normal size but happened to be crippled.

As a small child she'd had encephalitis—sleeping sickness. It had cut her down the middle, like a stroke. Her left arm was almost useless. She could walk, but she dragged her left leg, swinging it around from behind her with every step. When she was excited, which was especially the case when she made love, the paralyzed arm would start to quiver and then rise up, float upward, in a miraculous salute. She'd begin to swear like a sailor, cursing out of the side of her mouth, the side that wasn't thick with paralysis.

I stayed at her studio apartment once or twice a week, all the way through to morning. I almost always woke up before she did. Usually I worked on the newsletter for Beverly Home, while outside, in the desert clarity, people splashed in the apartment complex's tiny swimming pool. I sat at her dining table with pen and paper and consulted my notes, writing, "Special announcement! On Saturday, April 25th, at 6:30 p.m., a group from the Southern Baptist Church in Tollson will be putting on a Bible pageant for Beverly Home residents. It should be inspiring—don't miss it!"

She'd lie in bed a while, trying to stay asleep, clinging to that other world. But soon she'd get up, galumphing toward the bathroom with the sheet half wrapped around her and trailing her wildly orbiting leg. For the first few minutes after she got up in the morning her paralysis was quite a bit worse. It was unwholesome, and very erotic.

Once she was up we'd drink coffee, instant coffee with low-fat milk, and she'd tell me about all the boyfriends she'd had. She'd had more boyfriends than anybody I'd ever heard of. Most of them had been given short lives.

I liked the time we spent in her kitchen those mornings. She liked it, too. Usually we were naked. Her eyes shed a certain brightness while she talked. And then we made love.

Her sofabed was two steps from the kitchen. We'd take those steps and lie down. Ghosts and sunshine hovered around us. Memories, loved ones, everyone was watching. She'd had one boy-friend who was killed by a train—stalled on the tracks and thinking he could get his motor firing before the engine caught him, but he was wrong. Another fell through a thousand evergreen boughs in the north Arizona mountains, a tree surgeon or someone along those lines, and crushed his head. Two died in the Marines, one in Vietnam and the other, a younger boy, in an unexplained one-car accident just after basic training. Two black men: one died of too many drugs and another was shanked in prison—that means stabbed with a weapon from the wood-working shop. Most of these people, by the time they were dead, had long since left her to travel down their lonely paths. People just like us, but unluckier. I was full of a sweet pity for them as we lay in the sunny little room, sad that they would never live again, drunk with sadness, I couldn't get enough of it.

During my regular hours at Beverly Home, the full-time employees had their shift change, and a lot of them congregated, coming and going, in the kitchen, where the time clock was. I often went in there and flirted with some of the beau-tiful nurses. I was just learning to live sober, and in fact I was often confused, especially because some Antabuse I was taking was having a very uncharacteristic effect on me. Sometimes I heard voices muttering in my head, and a lot of the time the world seemed to smolder around its edges. But I was in a little better physical shape every day, I was getting my looks back, and my spirits were rising, and this was all in all a happy time for me.

All these weirdos, and me getting a little better every day right in the midst of them. I had never known, never even imagined for a heartbeat, that there might be a place for people like us.